YOUNG SAMSON

The Strongest Boy Who Ever Lived

YOUNG SAMSON

The Strongest Boy Who Ever Lived

by ISRAEL I. TASLITT

Illustrated by Luisada

A SABRA BOOK

FUNK AND WAGNALLS

NEW YORK

To

My grandsons, STEVEN and GARY,

My nephews, JONATHAN and SETH,

and all the young lads in the State of Israel today, each no less a Samson than the boy whom the spirit of the Lord moved, between Zor'ah and Eshtaol, thirty centuries ago, this book is affectionately dedicated.

I.I.T.

Contents

The Riddle-Master

THE INNKEEPER pushed aside the straw curtain and poked his head into the dining hall. At the rough wooden table a few guests were still dallying over their meal.

"Gluttons," he muttered under his breath. "Every last bite they must finish! One would think they had fasted all day. Stomachs they must have like bottomless caves!"

As if in echo of his words a low growl came from a corner of the room.

"Indeed you should be angry," the innkeeper remarked to the dog lying there, a mournful mongrel who appeared to have no faith at all in the future. "Not a scrap will they leave for you, those vultures, not even a bone to chew on."

The dog eyed his master wearily. It was the same old story, day after day: the guests leave nothing for you in the dining hall, and your master won't let you come into the kitchen. No dog could get fat on *that* kind of a diet. The mongrel rose slowly, shook his lean ribs into place, and headed for the door. Nothing to do but nose about the garbage pile again.

All at once the three guests at the table turned their heads, not at the sight of the dog slinking past them but at the newcomer in the doorway. He was slightly above average height and rather thin of frame. About his neck a gay scarf was tied loosely, but the cloak beneath it, besides being stained with dust, was tattered in spots. What attracted the others, from the moment that the stranger stepped into the hall, were his flashing dark eyes and short black beard.

"The proprietor of this establishment—where is he?" the newcomer called out in a ringing voice.

"Here I am, stranger," the innkeeper replied, wiping his hands on a dingy apron. "What do you want, food or lodging?"

"Both, my dear man," replied the newcomer. He advanced into the room. "I am on my way to Eshtaol, and this inn speaks to me of rest and refreshment."

The innkeeper's gaze measured the stranger from head to toe. "You have the price, I suppose?" he demanded. "One piece of silver for lodging in the common room. Two if you want a room of your own."

The other waved his hand modestly. "Ah, my dear man," he chuckled, "am I then a prince of royal blood to deserve quarters of my own? 'Tis enough if the bed is soft, and the food is tasty, and the entertainment good."

The three guests broke into laughter, much amused not only by the stranger's grand manner but also by the blank look on the face of the innkeeper.

"What?" the latter managed to gasp. "Entertainment? Hah! You may not be of royal blood, indeed, but your tongue talks like it would be in a king's mouth. Entertainment! Dancing girls, perhaps, or acrobats?"

"Calm yourself, my dear innkeeper," replied the stranger. "Not dancers nor acrobats, to be sure, but—why not a riddle-master?"

"Aha!" cried the innkeeper triumphantly. "So that's what you are—a wandering riddle-master, with words aplenty but without as much as a single silver coin, I wager."

The stranger bowed. "Our innkeeper is truly a man of wisdom. Allow me to introduce myself. Khiddon is my name, gentlemen; from Gilead across the Jordan. Were I not so modest I would admit to being the best riddle-master in the land. Indeed, from the Great Sea to the west and across to the hills of Moab, where rises the sun, the name of Khiddon is known wherever riddles are appreciated."

One of the guests snorted. "We of Ramah have not heard of you, O modest one."

"Ah, Ramah," sighed Khiddon. "'Tis indeed one of the few towns that I yet have not favored with my presence. But despair not, my good man. In time I shall be there, to pit my riddles against the brains of its inhabitants. Indeed, you may announce to your townsmen that Khiddon will be among them before the moon is full again."

"Bah!" exclaimed the man from Ramah. "Your riddles a child will solve."

"Shall I then set one before you?" Khiddon quickly suggested. He put his hand inside his cloak and brought forth two silver coins. "These are yours," he said, "if you solve it. If not, you shall pay our worthy innkeeper for my food and lodging."

"Agreed, agreed," the other guests shouted.

But the man from Ramah was not easily moved. "Wait, wait," he exclaimed. "I know these riddle-masters well. They pose riddles that one can hardly understand, then give answers that make no sense at all. I will agree only if your answer satisfies me—that is, if I do not solve your riddle in the first place."

Khiddon drew himself up haughtily. "Sir," he cried in an aggrieved tone, "your remarks about my profession are indeed unworthy, yet because your riddle-masters in Ramah are obviously of a poor sort I shall overlook your words." Once more he smiled at the group before him. "Listen then to my riddle, and may your brains be in good order. What is it, my dear people, that lies closest to your minds, night and day?"

The guests looked at each other blankly, while the innkeeper scratched his round head.

"How about it, my dear innkeeper?" Khiddon addressed him. "Will you pay me five pieces of silver a day to entertain your guests, with food and lodging?"

The man from Ramah, chagrined by his failure to solve the riddle, did not give the innkeeper a chance to reply. "Out with it, O riddle-master," he cried. "What is it that lies closest to my mind, night and day?"

Khiddon shrugged. "Your ears, do they not?"

The innkeeper and his guests were stunned, as though someone had swept a wet towel across their faces, but before anyone could recover, a young girl rushed into the room.

"Help!" she cried. "Help my father!"

The innkeeper hastened to her side. "What has happened, Ophrah?" he demanded.

"The cart fell on him," sobbed the girl. "He is under it."

The innkeeper threw off his apron. "Where is he?"

"Just beyond the mill."

Darkness was just falling as the innkeeper, followed by the others, hastened toward the scene of the accident. Already several townspeople had gathered about the overturned vehicle, and the groans of the man pinned beneath it filled the air.

Then, as if by magic, the groaning stopped. When Khiddon, now running ahead of his companions, reached the spot he stopped short in amazement. The injured man was being slowly pulled out. Holding up the cart, as if it were no more than a toy, was a young lad.

"See?" shouted the innkeeper into Ophrah's ear above the cheers of the crowd. "It is your father's good fortune that Samson happened to be about."

The girl knelt down by her father's side.

"His hurt is not heavy," one of the men assured her. "We shall take him home, while you hurry and fetch the physician."

Khiddon drew the innkeeper aside. "That boy!" he whispered excitedly. "Never have I seen such strength, not in one twice his age. Who is he?"

The innkeeper, now that the danger was over, eyed the riddle-master with open disdain. "Riddles you can ask, but what everyone knows is a riddle to you. When you go back to Gilead, tell the people that you have seen Samson of Zor'ah, of the tribe of Dan. Now, if you will pay me for your food and lodging, come to my inn. But no more riddles!"

Khiddon hardly heard the innkeeper's last remarks. His eyes were on Samson. Except for the long hair that spilled across the nape of his neck and down past his shoulders, there seemed to be nothing unusual about the boy. The shapeless leather mantle that he wore served to hide whatever strength might have otherwise been visible.

Samson gave the now upright cart a slight shake to test its firmness, then began to walk away. Instantly Khiddon was at his side.

"A word with you, young man," the riddle-master said. "Not in my native Gilead nor elsewhere in my travels have I come upon such a show of strength."

He paused, but Samson made no reply. He gave his companion a quick glance and walked on.

Khiddon decided to try a new tack. "I am a stranger in this town," he said softly. "Money I have little and the road before me is long. If there be a corner in your father's house, perhaps—"

Samson slowed his pace somewhat. "You are from across the Jordan?" he asked.

"Yes, I am a Reubenite," Khiddon replied. He wondered at Samson's voice; it was not as deep as a grown man's, but it sounded older than he had expected. "We have fine pastures in Gilead," he continued, eager to hold Samson's interest, "and balm to heal wounds, but no one as strong—"

"Come with me, then," Samson interrupted. "My parents will not turn you away."

Khiddon's heart felt lighter. "Ah, the spirit of grace certainly dwells among the people of Dan," he exclaimed. "May the blessings of heaven descend on your father's household."

No more was said as Samson led the way in the darkness past the low wood-and-stone houses that lined the winding street. From all sides came the small sounds of suppertime. One or two late arrivals from the fields hurried past the pair, eager to get home and enjoy the restful evening hours.

"That is where we live, over there," Samson pointed to a rambling stone house off to one side of the sandy road.

"It looks comfortable indeed," remarked Khiddon, unwittingly quickening his step. He had not eaten for the better part of the day. "You are sure that I won't be a burden to you and to your parents?" he added, watching Samson out of the corner of his eye.

"Who speaks of being a burden in my house?" came a voice from the doorway.

Khiddon looked hard at the man standing there. Despite the feeble light the riddle-master could see that the speaker, though sturdy of figure, was past his prime. For a moment Khiddon wondered whether he might not be Samson's grandfather.

"My son knows well that no guest is a burden," said the man, settling all doubts on that score. "Be he a wanderer or of the nobility, my home is open."

Khiddon bowed. "As many as are my thanks, so may God's blessings be upon you," he replied.

"Come break bread with us," Samson's father said, leading the way into the house.

A woman's voice came from somewhere inside. "Whom do you have there, Manoakh?"

"Samson has brought home a guest, my dear," her husband replied.

"A stranger?" Khiddon thought he detected a note of fear in the word.

"I am sure that we have enough for everyone," Manoakh said. He took hold of Khiddon's arm. "Come, I shall show you where there is water to wash away the dust of the road. Then we shall be seated, for the hour is late."

Samson's mother came toward them. She, too, seemed to be much older than Khiddon would have thought. About her shoulders was a black shawl, even though the night was far from cold.

The meal itself, after the style of the country towns, was simple but hearty. There was freshly churned butter for the roasted ears of corn, flat cakes spread with golden honey and a pitcher of cool milk.

No one spoke during the meal, but twice Khiddon caught the eyes of Samson's mother fixed upon him. In vain did the riddle-master try to fathom the meaning of her gaze.

"This is indeed the finest meal that I have eaten since leaving Gilead," he remarked gratefully. He washed down the last of the second cake with a final gulp of milk. "Indeed I am glad that my riddle did not please the innkeeper."

"Your riddle?" asked Manoakh.

"Ah, yes," returned Khiddon, blushing slightly. "How rude of me! I should have told you that I am a riddle-master, for such is the means by which I make my living. I was in the midst of confusing the innkeeper with one of my riddles when this girl came for help, to get her father out from under his overturned cart. When we reached the scene, there was your son, holding up the cart as if it were no more than a feather, and a light one at that, so that none was needed to give him a hand."

Samson rose. "I shall tend to the animals in the barn," he said, and left the house.

"This is how he always is," remarked Manoakh, sighing. "Mention his strength and he will find some reason not to be about."

Khiddon leaned forward. "Does it really bother him? His being so much stronger than others, I mean. Does he get to play with boys of his age, or do they keep away from him? And why does he wear his hair so long?"

Manoakh and his wife exchanged a brief glance. This was not the first time that such questions had been asked of them.

Khiddon understood at once what was in the mind of his hosts, but before he could say anything at all Samson's mother made a move as if to rise. "Perhaps our guest is tired," she suggested to her husband. "He may have to rise early in order to be on his way before the heat of the sun. I shall prepare his bed."

"No, no, not at all," Khiddon replied hastily. "I need little sleep. Should I go to bed now I would only lie awake for hours, fashioning riddles in my mind. And it may be that I shall need to deal with riddles no longer." He turned to Manoakh. "Sir," he said, and there was a note of firmness in his voice, "I know that there must be an unusual story to Samson and that you must have told the story often, to many people. Yet if I ask you to relate it to me, now, it is because I, too, have something of importance to say."

A slight gasp came from the woman at the table, but her face remained unmoved. Manoakh looked at her in surprise, then began:

"For many years my wife and I were childless, much to our sorrow. Others told us that we were fortunate, not to have children who would have to live under the Philistine yoke. Still we prayed to God for at least one son or daughter.

"One day, while I was working in the field, my wife came to me in great haste. A stranger had appeared before her. She was sure that he was a holy man, for his face shone with a light not given to human beings. He told her that she would give birth to a son—a most unusual boy. From his boyhood on he would have to keep away from many things. He would be sacred to God, said the stranger, although neither my wife nor I could understand what this meant. In the meantime, my wife was not to have any strong drink nor eat anything that was not pure, just as our son would have to do.

"Happy though I was to learn all this," continued Manoakh, "I was also much disturbed by it. Why was our son to be different from other children? Neither I nor my forefathers were anything but plain, simple people. I therefore prayed to God and asked that the holy man be sent to us again, so that he might tell us what we should do for the boy after he is born, and how to take care of him."

"And he came again?" asked Khiddon.

"He did," replied Manoakh. "This time he appeared to my wife when she was in the field. She called me and I spoke to the holy man. But he had nothing new to tell us. Again he warned my wife not to have anything that came from the fruit of the vine nor to eat anything impure."

"But he did not tell you why," commented Khiddon.

Manoakh shook his head. "By not so much as one word. He even refused to tell us his name. We offered to prepare a meal for him, but he refused, saying that whatever offering we wanted to make should be made to God. This we did, and as we placed our offering on the altar a sheet of flame came down before our eyes. When we could see again, the stranger was gone. Thus we knew that he was a messenger of God. We saw him no more, not before Samson's birth, nor afterwards."

Khiddon drew a deep breath. "This is absolutely the most amazing story I have ever heard."

Manoakh chuckled. "Well do I remember that day," he said. "I was sure that we would die on the spot, for we had seen the image of God, through his messenger. But my wife thought otherwise, probably because she was so excited about becoming a mother at last. 'If God would have wanted us to die,' she told me, 'He would not have accepted our offering, nor brought all this to pass before our very eyes, nor told us about all these things.' And indeed here we are, alive and well, with a son to be at our side as we get on in years."

Again Khiddon shook his head. "And that is how it really turned out?" he asked.

"We have obeyed the messenger's words as he had told us," Manoakh replied, "and all has come to pass as he had said."

"And you still don't know why Samson has to separate himself from the ways of others, or why he possesses such strength?" asked the riddle-master.

Manoakh shrugged, and neither man noticed that

Samson's mother was becoming more and more uneasy.

"I have something to propose to you," Khiddon went on. "The thought came to me in a flash, even as I was watching your son holding up the cart. By the way," he said, "if your son is sacred to God, what work is he allowed to do?"

"Nothing that brings gain to us," Manoakh replied. "He does help others, whether they are in distress or if they need help in the fields and cannot afford to pay for it, for these are acts of which God certainly approves."

"True indeed," said Khiddon. "Only it may be that your son can be of help not only to his neighbors here in Zor'ah but to the whole tribe of Dan."

This time there was no mistaking the cry of pain that came from the woman's lips. Manoakh bent toward her. "Are you ill?" he asked anxiously.

"No, no," she whispered. "Let the stranger speak."

Khiddon's eyebrows went up in surprise. "I meant nothing wrong," he hastened to say. "I was about to propose that you allow me to take Samson to see the world. We can go to my native Gilead, or even up among the Canaanites. He with his strength and I with my riddles—together we shall not only earn much money but shall also spread the fame of Zor'ah and of the tribe of Dan far and wide. This is what I had in mind."

Manoakh shook his head vigorously. "No, no," he exclaimed. "This cannot be. Our son is not a prize ox or a fatted calf to be shown before people. Besides, he is much too young for such travels. As for money, remember that he is sacred to God, and wealth is not for him."

"True, true," sighed Khiddon. Suddenly a gleam shot

into his eyes like a bolt of lightning. "I have it!" he cried. "Samson and I shall go neither to Gilead nor to the land of the Canaanites. No! We shall go to Ashkelon, Ashdod, Gaza—"

"What!" cried Manoakh, jumping up as though bitten by a snake. "You will take our son to the cities of the Philistines, into the lairs of our enemies and oppressors? Your senses must have taken leave of you, sir! If it were not that you are our guest—"

"Yes, my husband! Samson shall go to Philistia!"

Both men stared wide-eyed at Samson's mother. She had risen to her feet, and was quivering as in a chill wind.

Manoakh was immediately at her side, his arms about her shaking shoulders. "Be calm, my dear," he said soothingly. "Tell me what is troubling you."

Slowly the woman sank back to her seat. "I have always feared this moment," she whispered, "but I knew that it had to come. Come near to me, Manoakh."

Khiddon also bent a little closer, for the woman's voice was very faint.

"There was something that the messenger of God told me which he did not repeat when he came again," she went on. "I never mentioned it to you, Manoakh, because I knew that it would worry you. I therefore vowed to keep silent until someone else would utter it first."

"Utter what first?" asked Manoakh.

"About Samson and the Philistines," his wife replied. "After God's messenger had told me that Samson would be sacred to God, and that his hair should never be shorn, he also gave me the reason. Our son, Manoakh, is to save our people from the Philistines."

A dead silence descended on the room. Manoakh kept staring at his wife, not knowing whether to believe his ears or not.

It was Khiddon who finally spoke. "Believe me, Manoakh," he said earnestly. "I am not a holy man, much less a messenger of the Lord. I spoke about taking Samson to Philistia as—well, as a venture to earn some money, and so did I mean it. But what your good wife has just told us does make sense, Manoakh. For what purpose was Samson given his strength? You have said that he uses it to help others. What greater help can he give than to free his people from Philistine rule? And who is more fitted for this task than one of the tribe of Dan, which has been suffering the most? Indeed, it must have been the will of the Lord that led my feet to Zor'ah."

Manoakh did not reply at once. He rose slowly and went to the doorway. He looked up at the heavens, hidden behind the twinkling stars. From the fields came the chirping of crickets, and the howl of a lonely jackal echoed in the night.

"This, then, is the reason," Manoakh said, half to himself. "Our son is to lift the burden which has been oppressing us all these years. Let it be thus, if it is the will of the Lord." He turned to Khiddon. "Take him with you, O riddle-master," he whispered. "But watch over him. He belongs to the Lord, yet he is also all *we* have."

Samson's mother did not say a word, but down her wrinkled cheeks the tears came streaming freely.

In the early hours of the following day Khiddon was awakened by the sound of excited voices on the other side of the wall. He listened intently, but other than the repeated mention of "sheep" and "lion" the conversation was blurred.

In front of the house Khiddon found Manoakh and Samson surrounded by a group of country folk. The voices died down as the riddle-master came near.

"Speak freely," Manoakh said to the others. "He is a trusted guest."

"We are at our wits' end, Manoakh," one of them exclaimed. "Every day it's a lamb, a sheep, even a calf. Now we know where this mountain lion has its lair, but what can we do? There is none among us either brave or foolish enough to risk his life."

Manoakh frowned. "And you want Samson to teach the beast a lesson, is that it?" he demanded.

The farmer scratched his head. "We are your neighbors," he replied, "and we cannot think of any other way to hunt the lion down, only by Samson's use of his strength in some way."

All this time Samson had been standing silently, his eyes on the ground. Now he raised his head. "I am not a hunter," he said quietly, "but if you know where this lion has its lair, I am willing to try."

A shout of approval rose from the group.

"Where is this lair?" asked Samson.

"In a cave," replied the farmer, "among the ravines on the other side of Makhne-Dan, a few hundred paces off the road to Eshtaol."

Khiddon spoke up for the first time. "Ah, 'tis to Eshtaol that I, too, am going. I am skilled with the bow and arrow. Perhaps I can be of help."

The farmer laughed. "A bow and arrow, you say? Let me tell you, sir, that this lion is so fast that he can dodge any arrow that is shot at him."

Manoakh in the meantime was studying Khiddon's face. Eshtaol was to the east; Philistia lay to the south. Then he understood. No one was to know that Samson was about to journey to the Philistine cities.

"Lead me to a spot where I can see the cave," Samson said. "Then we shall decide what is to be done."

It was almost noon when the group passed through Makhne-Dan. Ahead rose the hills and the road to Jebus, the fortified capital of the Jebusites. Here and there winding trails branched off the main road and disappeared into the wooded patches of the foothills.

"Up this way," one of the farmers pointed.

Here the ground began to rise sharply. Underfoot the rock-studded earth made the going even more difficult. The group skirted several large boulders that leaned into the trail until a deep crevice in the ground loomed up ahead. It kept growing wider, then broadened into a gully, dry and stony, some forty paces across.

"There," said the farmer who acted as the guide. "Look down there, near that clump of bushes, about three paces to the right."

Khiddon and Samson followed the guide's pointing finger. Half-hidden by the scrubby growth was the dark opening of a small cave.

"We could close up the opening," the guide remarked, "but then the lion would find another cave. Besides, he might decide to be around while we are there."

"True enough," Khiddon agreed. He turned to

Samson. "What do you have in mind?"

Samson appeared to be studying not the cave but the spot on which he and the others were standing. The ground here, hardened by the sun, was as firm as the reddish boulders of all sizes that lay strewn along the edge of the gully.

Without another word Samson set about gathering up the larger boulders, most of which were too heavy to be lifted by an ordinary person. These he placed one on top of the other at the very lip of the crevice, directly across from the cave. "Would the lion be in its lair now?" he asked.

The guide shook his head. "That robber doesn't come back until later in the afternoon, usually with one of our lambs between his jaws. We better get out of the sun and sit in the shade until he comes."

For once the farmer was wrong. Hardly had he spoken the last words when the object of the hunt came into view, loping easily along the bottom of the gully. And from the lion's jaws hung a limp lamb.

"Let him enter the cave," Samson said quietly. He picked up one of the smaller boulders and stationed himself just to the left of the stone pile. Then, cradling the boulder in the crook of his arm as in a sling, he sent it spinning high across the gully toward the mouth of the cave. As soon as the boulder crashed into the ground, not more than five paces from its target, Samson heaved the whole wall of stones after it.

At the sound of the first boulder the lion came hurtling from the cave. But he did not get far. Before he could flee out of reach the stone shower was upon him. He let out a blood-curdling roar, then quivered and lay still, buried beneath the pile.

A shout of glee went up from the farmers. They crowded about Samson, each trying to outdo the others in thanking the boy for his feat. But Samson, as Khiddon noted, did not appear to enjoy his victory over the beast. He kept looking at the pile of boulders as though it were a monument not to his own strength but to the animal lying dead beneath it.

As the farmers clambered down the slope of the gully for the trophy of the dead lion, Khiddon put his hand on the boy's shoulder. "I know your heart, Samson," he said gently. "You are thinking that it took only strength, but not courage, to do what you have done. Do not despair," he laughed grimly, "for you will soon be using both, in the land of the Philistines!"

Walking Dagon

THE MEN trudging along the road to Ashdod looked like a band of ghosts, in the early hours of a misty dawn. Heads lowered, they kept hard on each other's heels, in a shuffling step that grated harshly on the hard-packed sand.

At first glance these travelers appeared to be beggars, right from the torn straw covering atop their matted hair to the tattered sandals on their feet. But the grim look on their faces and the tight line of their lips were not the signs of the alms-seekers. The shadowy travelers were more like men going into battle than paupers on the run.

Khiddon and Samson, astride their mules, caught up with the band a short distance from the Philistine city, just as the rising sun was beginning to dispel the mist. They were about to pass the silent group when one of the travelers suddenly sank to the ground, clutching at his chest in agony. Before any of his companions could make a move, Khiddon was at the side of the stricken man. In his hand the riddle-master had his goatskin wine pouch.

"Stand away," he commanded, loosening the frayed coat of the man on the ground. With a quick motion he brought the pouch to the man's lips and forced the liquid through between them. The traveler choked a little, gasped and tried to sit up.

"Lie still, you!" growled Khiddon. "One sip of strong

drink and the lamb wants to be a lion." He rose to his feet. "Carry him to the side of the road," he ordered. "After a while he will be able to ride on my mule to Ashdod—if that is where you people are going."

The others nodded dully and set about to do Khiddon's bidding, but one of them remained behind. "My name is Kafri," he introduced himself to the riddle-master.

"We are from the village of Kurat, to the north. I want to thank you, stranger. Not many would have stopped to do an act of kindness to such as we are."

Khiddon made the pouch fast to the mule's trappings. "Think nothing of it, friend," he replied. "We all travel along one road."

Kafri gave Khiddon a searching look. "You are not a Philistine," he observed, "neither do you talk like a Canaanite."

"As I have said, we all travel one road," the riddle-master said shortly. "You are headed for Ashdod?"

"Yes," replied Kafri. "Ashdod is our destination. Is it yours?"

"It is on our way," responded Khiddon. "My young companion and I are passing through Philistia, to see its cities and to meet its people. If we find Ashdod interesting we shall tarry there for a day or two. If not, we shall turn our steps elsewhere."

Some of the villagers had gathered close, and Khiddon thought he saw them exchange guarded glances.

"Have you ever heard the name Shabbal?" Kafri asked, and again Khiddon felt that he was about to learn something strange. "No," he replied. "Who is this Shabbal?"

"You are indeed not from this part of the country if you have never heard of Shabbal," was the reply. "He is the nephew of Amredat."

"Amredat—Amredat," repeated Khiddon. "Is he not the ruler of Ashdod?"

"The ruler of Ashdod he is," returned Kafri grimly, "and the oppressor of the poor. He has made our taxes heavy and our lot miserable. If we cannot pay the taxes he forces us to toil on the docks, with no gain for us and only bread and water to keep us alive. For our work he collects much gold from the ships that come into the harbor."

"And Shabbal?" asked Khiddon. "Where is his place in all this?"

"Ah, Shabbal!" cried Kafri with deep feeling. "As day is unlike night, as the summer sun is unlike the winter storm, so is Shabbal unlike his uncle, the tyrant. Amredat's heart is made of stone; Shabbal is kindness itself. Shabbal has always cried out against Amredat's treatment of the poor."

"And his uncle has allowed this to take place?" wondered Khiddon.

The villagers snickered. "At first," continued Kafri, "Amredat paid no attention to his nephew. Let the young calf moo his poems in the market place! Besides, Shabbal's father had died a hero's death in a raid on the Egyptian border, while he, Amredat, was busy collecting taxes from the poor."

"How old is Shabbal?" asked Khiddon. "He must be young enough to be foolish and old enough to be brave."

"He came of age only a month ago," replied Kafri. "On that day he threw away his poems and began to speak out like a grown man. Every word was a demand that Amredat cease oppressing us. But on the very next day the tyrant issued a warning to Shabbal that he keep silent or be sent into exile. This Shabbal has refused to do. And today, if Shabbal speaks again in the market place, Amredat has vowed to punish him severely, nephew or no nephew."

Khiddon looked at the villagers. "And you are going to Ashdod to save Shabbal from his fate?"

Kafri sighed deeply. "No, my friend, this we cannot do," he replied. "We have no arms in the villages. The blacksmiths will fashion weapons only for the rich and for the captains of war. If we make any move to help Shabbal the soldiers will cut us down without mercy. But we still want to be in Ashdod, at the market place. If Shabbal obeys his uncle, then we shall accept our fate or move away from Amredat's territory."

"And if Shabbal ignores his uncle's decree?" asked Khiddon.

"Then," replied Kafri, lowering his voice, "we shall not rest until Amredat will suffer greater punishment than whatever he will inflict on Shabbal."

Khiddon looked around until he caught Samson's eye. The boy was standing with the mules, but his ears had heard every word that had been said. He now answered Khiddon's look with a slight nod. Yes, the Philistines were oppressing not only the tribe of Dan but their own poor as well.

Khiddon turned his gaze toward the spot where the

stricken villager was lying. "Your comrade seems to have recovered," he remarked to Kafri. "Two of you lift him on to the mule and hold him steady until we reach Ashdod."

NEWS OF what was going to take place in Amredat's city had spread from one end of Philistia to the other. All the roads leading into Ashdod were choked with eager throngs, hurrying to be on hand to witness the contest between Shabbal and his uncle.

All this was not to the liking of Amredat and his advisers; the less people the better, they thought. But Reshak the High Priest argued otherwise. If Shabbal was to be silenced, he told Amredat, then let all Philistia know it; if not, then why go through with the plan at all? At last Amredat and the others agreed and the gates to the city were allowed to remain open. At the same time Amredat made sure that his soldiers were stationed everywhere.

Once inside the gates, Khiddon and Samson bade farewell to Kafri and his villagers. They made the mules comfortable in the courtyard of a nearby inn and set out for the market place in the center of the city.

"We shall not get very far," remarked Khiddon, eyeing the huge crowd that had already gathered. "Let us find a food stall, else we might faint from hunger and miss everything."

The two were still munching on their bread and cheese when a loud cheer broke from the crowd. Shabbal, dressed in a loose cloak of coarse gray cloth, was slowly making his way toward the town well at the center of the market area. The throng gave way before him, cheering wildly at every step.

Suddenly the blast of a horn rose above the cheers. From the opposite direction came a covered chariot, its iron wheels rattling on the hard ground. A line of mounted guards rode on either side of the chariot, bare swords glistening in the sunlight. There were no cheers from the crowd now, as the bystanders pressed back to make room for the chariot.

"These Ashdodians do not like their ruler," Samson remarked. He and Khiddon were almost directly in the path of the oncoming vehicle.

The riddle-master shook his head. "One cannot tell," he retorted. "The folks here in the market place are mostly Shabbal's followers. The others are no doubt seeking the shelter of their homes."

"You think that there is trouble ahead?" asked Samson eagerly.

"Hah! I am sure of it," replied Khiddon. "If Shabbal had any thought of giving in to his uncle he would have simply disappeared, or at least kept away from the market place today. His presence means that he intends to defy Amredat."

"Shabbal must indeed be a brave man," said Samson. "I wish I could help him."

Khiddon held up his hand in warning. "Do nothing rash, Samson," he said sternly. "With all these guards around, anyone making a move to help Shabbal will be cut down at once. Then, too, we must not attract attention to ourselves. This is a matter for the people of Ashdod to settle."

But as if in challenge to Khiddon's words a strange

thing happened. One of the guards at the head of the chariot let his sword fall loose from his grip. The sharp weapon landed, point down, on the back of one of the two horses pulling the chariot. The horse jumped, then reared back on its hind legs, tilting the chariot to one side so steeply that the driver tumbled off his high perch to the ground. The other horse, also thoroughly frightened, squirmed wildly in its traces. In the meantime the guards, struggling to keep the chariot upright, hemmed the vehicle in so tightly that Amredat remained a prisoner inside.

It was at this point that Samson, unmindful of Khiddon's warning, sprang forward toward the bewildered animals. One leap carried him high up to the shaft between them. With almost the same motion he sank his fingers into the horses' manes and swung back to the ground, bringing the animals down with him with such force that they remained stunned and trembling with fright.

For a moment Shabbal was forgotten, and a silent spell seemed to settle on the throng. The guards pulled away from the chariot. Amredat, his dark face still flushed from the shock, climbed down from the chariot and strode toward Samson.

"Your name?" he asked, his eyes sweeping over the boy's sturdy figure. Here indeed was a lad he could use!

Khiddon managed to wriggle close to Amredat. "The boy is my nephew," he exclaimed glibly. "We are from Ammonite territory, beyond the Jordan to the north, and it is our king himself who favors the boy."

"So!" returned Amredat gruffly, much disappointed.

The king of the Ammonites was not one to be trifled with, as Ashdod's ruler well knew. He reached inside his cloak and brought forth a gold coin. "Here, spend it on your nephew," he said, flipping it toward Khiddon and returning to the chariot.

The charioteer had in the meantime clambered back up to his seat, amid the jeers of the crowd. He looked down, saw that Amredat was back inside the chariot, and motioned to Samson to let go of the horses. Once, twice he flicked his whip at their backs, but the animals would not move. Again he used his whip, and again they refused to budge.

"The curse of Baal-Zebub be upon you," the driver yelled. This time he lashed at the horses so savagely that the whip flew out of his hand.

Khiddon saw his opportunity. "The horses are frightened, driver," he called up to the enraged charioteer. "Let me show you how we of Ammon handle even the wildest among them." Without waiting for the driver's reply he clambered up, motioning to Samson to do the same. This way both of them would have the best view of whatever was going to take place between Shabbal and his uncle.

The riddle-master took the reins out of the charioteer's hands and let them flap ever so gently on the backs of the quivering horses. "Be not afraid, my beauties," he called out softly. "Let us go, so that the exalted ruler of Ashdod may render judgment in his wisdom, which shall shine forth like the sun in its course across the heavens!"

Those in the crowd within earshot of Khiddon's grand words exchanged looks of amazement. Who was

this stranger, and who was this mighty nephew of his?

But this was no time for guessing. At the first sound of Khiddon's voice the horses pricked up their ears. Their quivering stopped, and a moment later the chariot was moving forward, pace after pace, until it came to a halt at the well.

And now the guards moved swiftly. They pushed their way through the crowd and formed a sword-bristling circle around Shabbal and the chariot.

Amredat stepped to the ground. His face, set in hard lines, showed no trace of emotion. He cast a brief glance at the tense crowd pressing around him and strode forward, until only the width of the well was between him and his kinsman.

"I have dealt well and patiently with you, Shabbal my nephew," he began in a loud voice. "I offered you to be a leader among men, like your father who was my younger brother. I wanted you to live with me in the palace, so that you may one day be my heir, since I am childless. But you have chosen to turn a deaf ear to my words and a heart of stone to my offer. This has brought me much pain."

A subdued titter ran through the crowd. Everyone knew that Amredat had offered his nephew the post of tax-collector in the villages around Ashdod, a post which he well knew that Shabbal would never accept.

"Instead of accepting my kind offer," Amredat went on, raising his voice even higher, "you have been behaving in ill fashion toward me. You have been accusing me of oppressing the poor. Yet if such were the case, why have not the poor gone to live in Gath or in Ashkelon or in the villages around Gaza? No, my dear nephew, no! You have chosen to blacken my name in the eyes of my people because you wish them to rise against me, so that you may become the ruler of Ashdod, even before I lie with my fathers!"

It was a good speech, thought Khiddon, but, looking around, he saw that it had made little impression on the crowd.

Amredat did not take his eyes off his nephew. "Had your father not been my brother," he continued, "I would have long dealt with you as you deserve. Also because you are young I am ready to forgive you, if in the hearing of the good people of Ashdod, my loyal subjects, you will now promise to cease your prattle and to hold your peace. I have spoken."

An uneasy stir passed through the crowd. In the presence of his powerful uncle, and with the ring of swords about him, what would Shabbal do?

But when the young man in the gray cloak spoke, it was not to Amredat but to the throng that pressed around him on every side.

"Yes, my uncle, Amredat the ruler of Ashdod, has spoken," Shabbal cried, flinging out his arm. "Why do not the poor people of Ashdod and its villages go elsewhere in Philistia, if things are indeed so bad for them here? I shall tell you why—it is because everywhere in Philistia there are others who would deny them the right to live in peace and happiness."

The scowl deepened on Amredat's face. If Shabbal's words were to reach the ears of the rulers of the other Philistine cities . . .

"And yet," continued Shabbal, his dark eyes flashing, "it is not for me to cry out against the injustice being done to the poor in Gaza or Ashkelon, though my heart goes out to them and my sleep is disturbed by their sad state. But I am an Ashdodian, and here I shall demand that the poor be allowed to live in peace and to keep the fruits of their labors."

Khiddon glanced at Samson. The boy was gazing at Shabbal with open admiration. As for himself, Khiddon was not yet ready to make up his mind about the young man. He sounded sincere, to be sure, and there was no doubt that he had the courage to stand up to his uncle.

But Amredat, much to everyone's amazement, did not order his soldiers to haul Shabbal off to the palace dungeon. Instead, a smile appeared on his face.

"Ah, Shabbal my nephew," he exclaimed. "You are just like your father, my dear brother—stubborn, fiery, always ready to champion those who cannot help themselves. Who am I, then, to say whether you are right or wrong? I shall not even attempt it. Let them who are mightier, and wiser, make the decision. I therefore decree that, tonight, you shall have your fate decided by Walking Dagon himself!"

A gasp went up from the crowd, and the market place began to hum as with a thousand beehives. Khiddon and Samson waited for more to come.

But nothing happened. It seemed that, once Amredat had pronounced the words "Walking Dagon," everyone knew exactly what was to follow.

The soldiers at the well surrounded Shabbal and led him off to the chariot. The young man climbed into it calmly and took his seat beside his uncle.

The charioteer was already turning the vehicle around when he noticed that Khiddon and Samson were still with him.

"Is it too much to ask," said Khiddon, before the driver could open his mouth, "that we be allowed to see the palace grounds, before we leave Ashdod? After all, we were of some service to your master."

The driver frowned. He didn't know what to make of the two strangers. Still, there was no denying that they had helped Amredat escape what might have been a serious state of affairs.

"Stay on," he replied gruffly. "But you are to be gone by the time the horses are in the stable."

It did not take the chariot long to get back to the palace. The packed throng in the market place had melted away as though a hot wind had blown it apart.

Amredat leaped to the ground before the chariot had come to a halt. "Guard this one well," he said to one of the soldiers, "and summon Reshak to my quarters at once."

The driver watched his master disappear into the squat stone structure. "It will be another one of those nights," he muttered.

"You do not sound pleased," remarked Khiddon. "Is some trouble in store for you?"

"Trouble?" repeated the driver. "Trouble enough. Again I will not be able to sleep until long after midnight. Then up again I have to be at sunrise."

"Indeed?" cried Khiddon. "Amredat is a hard taskmaster, then?"

The driver slapped vainly at a fly that kept buzzing about his head. "From morning till nightfall is bad enough," he grumbled, "but when Dagon walks I must suffer."

"Walking Dagon, eh?" asked Khiddon. "Who—or rather, what is it?"

The driver looked at the riddle-master with undisguised ire. "You want to make me believe that you've never heard of Walking Dagon? Either you think I'm a child or it must be that you're a fool."

"No offense, no offense," Khiddon hastily cried. "Indeed we have come from afar, from the land of the Ammonites. Many wonderful things have we heard about the Philistines, yet not so much as a word about Walking Dagon."

"So!" exclaimed the driver. He seemed to be immensely pleased; here was someone—two of them—who had never heard about Walking Dagon! What an opportunity for a good storyteller!

"Walking Dagon," began the driver, "is a statue which Reshak the High Priest has in his garden. At his bidding it walks."

"Just like that?" exclaimed Khiddon.

"Just like that," replied the driver, enjoying the other's surprise.

"Amazing," returned Khiddon. "Now tell me, when and where does this Dagon walk?"

"Not often," replied the driver. "Only when there is an important dispute to be settled in Ashdod. If Amredat feels that he cannot settle the matter, he calls on Walking Dagon to do it."

Khiddon whistled softly. "And how does Walking Dagon do it?"

"Aha!" exclaimed the driver triumphantly. "I knew you'd ask that. Let me therefore tell you. On any night that Amredat calls for a trial by Walking Dagon, which takes place just past the second watch, the whole town turns out at the sporting field, outside the city walls. The two parties stand opposite each other, Reshak reads the case, and Walking Dagon walks toward the guilty one."

Khiddon turned towards Samson. "Tell me, my dear nephew," he exclaimed. "In all your young days, have you ever heard anything so amazing as the story which our friend here has told so well?"

Samson solemnly shook his head. "Never," he replied. "Never in my young life have I ever heard such an amazing story."

The driver was all smiles. Never had he enjoyed such a grateful audience. "Yes, it is indeed amazing," he went on. "Of course, only Reshak can make Walking Dagon do his bidding, for Reshak is the High Priest of Ashdod, and he possesses many powers."

"Without doubt," commented Khiddon. "But tell me, how does Walking Dagon know which of the two parties is the guilty one? Are there witnesses testifying at the trial?"

The driver gave Khiddon a sour look. "That is nonsense!" he exclaimed. "Is it not enough that Dagon walks—you also want him to hear?"

"No, no," Khiddon replied hastily. "Walking is enough of a miracle for Dagon, and I would not think of demanding that he should also be able to hear. Now, then, you say that Dagon walks toward the guilty one. What then?"

"Then," said the driver, "Amredat calls out the punishment which the guilty one is to suffer." He looked around cautiously. "Do you want to know a secret?" he whispered.

Both Khiddon and Samson leaned closer. "Tell us," the riddle-master urged. "With us any secret is safe, especially if you tell it to us."

"Very well," replied the driver. "I shall tell you what everyone in Ashdod thinks—but does not say with his lips. Dagon has never yet walked toward anyone known to be favored by Amredat!"

"Ah, indeed you have a keen mind," said Khiddon. "Then you think that there is some trick to Walking Dagon?"

"No, no," exclaimed the driver fearfully, again looking about. "It must be that Amredat has friends who are never guilty." He shook his head. "No, it is not a trick. More than once did Amredat insist that the statue be examined, before it walked and after it walked, and never was any trickery found."

Khiddon sighed. "Surely it is wonderful to be an Ashdodian and be in the presence of Walking Dagon," he remarked, much to Samson's amusement. "Therefore one should not be angry if the trial causes loss of sleep."

The driver's eyes opened wide. "You are right!" he exclaimed. "I've never thought of it that way."

"Indeed," replied Khiddon. He gave the driver a friendly pat on the back. "Fortunate is Amredat to have one like you in his service." He motioned to Samson and together they walked out through the gate, leaving the driver very much pleased with himself.

The two set out for the market place again. Khiddon was silent for some time, and Samson, feeling sure that something was at work in the riddle-master's mind, didn't say a word.

"This Walking Dagon has aroused my curiosity," Khiddon finally said, "I think we ought to look into the matter."

"What do you intend to do?" asked Samson.

"I am not sure," Khiddon replied slowly. "It depends on what we shall learn. Right now we shall go back to the spot where you stopped the horses." His tone became serious. "That was a rash thing to do, Samson," he chided, "though brave enough."

"I did it without thinking," Samson said, his face reddening.

"True, true," Khiddon said kindly. "I expect that it will do us much good—right now." He nodded toward the row of shops ahead. "That is where I think we shall learn more about Walking Dagon."

It did not take Samson long to understand Khiddon's plan. No sooner did they stop at the first counter than the shopkeeper hurried toward them, beaming with delight.

"Ah, 'tis the brave boy who mastered Amredat's horses," he exclaimed. "You are indeed blessed with great strength."

Khiddon, delighted with the opening that the shopkeeper had given him, waved his hand airily. "That was but child's play, my dear man," he exclaimed. "May

I inform you that my nephew here is stronger than any grown man in Philistia!"

The smile vanished from the shopkeeper's face. "Those are bold words, O boastful one," he growled. "You speak as though every strong man in Philistia is known to you."

Khiddon shrugged haughtily. "It matters not, my dear man," he replied. "Show me any man of strength in Ashdod, and my nephew will outdo him—easily, without effort, without one grunt."

The shopkeeper burst into loud laughter. "Ah, you are indeed a proud and vain uncle," he cried. "Your heart speaks with love for the boy, but your tongue drowns it out with ignorance. Let me tell you, my friend, that Ashdod abounds with strong men. There is Makish, for instance. Do you know what Makish can do?"

"What," asked Khiddon bitingly, "can Makish do?"

"Makish," replied the shopkeeper solemnly, "can take a stone three times as large as your fist and crush it between his hands into dust. That, my friend, is what Makish can do."

"Very interesting," commented Khiddon calmly. "Only my nephew here can take dust and press it between his hands with such strength that it turns into stone."

The shopkeeper shot Samson a startled glance, and the boy, wondering what Khiddon was up to, did his best to smile modestly.

"And who else is strong in Ashdod?" Khiddon prodded.

The shopkeeper did not look pleased, but he went on. "Then there is Merim. But Betan is the strongest of all.

I hesitate to tell you what Betan can do, for you will not believe it."

"Tell me, tell me," urged Kiddon. "After I hear what you have to say about this Betan I shall know whether to believe you or not."

"Very well," retorted the shopkeeper briskly. "Let me tell you what Betan can do. Betan will get down to his knees and place his hands on the ground, palms up. Then he will have one man sit down on one palm and another man on the other. He will then lift both men up, rise to his feet, and lift both men high over his head, holding them there while your heart beats ten times. Do you need more proof?"

Khiddon sighed and put his hand on the shopkeeper's shoulder. "My friend," he declared, "I must admit that never have I heard of such strength as that which your Betan possesses. Now tell me, what does one of Betan's strength do here in Ashdod? Or does he go traveling about the country, seeking challengers to his prowess?"

"Ho, ho, such questions!" exclaimed the shopkeeper merrily. "What else should Betan do but serve Amredat?"

"Serve Amredat, you say?" asked Khiddon. "How?"

The shopkeeper became impatient. "How? How? you ask. How should I know? It may be that he teaches feats of strength to the guards. One thing I can tell you, stranger; he does not spend his time picking flowers."

Khiddon nudged Samson to join in with the shop-keeper's laughter at his own humor. "Well, we shall bid you goodbye now," he said. "Soon Ashdod and its many attractions will be behind us."

The shopkeeper opened his mouth in surprise.

"What?" he exclaimed. "Are you not going to witness the trial?"

Khiddon shook his head sadly. "I am afraid that we must be on our way, though the thought of seeing all that is to be seen is certainly tempting." He leaned toward the shopkeeper. "But since we shall not be at the trial, perhaps you will tell us how it is conducted. Then we can spread the story of Walking Dagon in our native land, beyond the Jordan."

The shopkeeper needed no further encouragement. "Walking Dagon," he began, "is carried from Reshak's home to the sporting grounds by twelve priests, which should give you an idea of its weight. It is set down in the center of the field. The other priests who come in with Walking Dagon then do the Dance of Justice, until Reshak tells them to stop."

"Reshak then conducts the trial?" asked Khiddon, just to make sure that the shopkeeper's story agreed with the driver's.

"Of course," returned the shopkeeper. "He is the High Priest, and Dagon walks only at his bidding and no one else's." He paused. "Now where was I?"

"Reshak has just told the priests to stop dancing," prompted Khiddon.

"Exactly," declared the shopkeeper. "Reshak then proclaims the matter of the trial and asks Walking Dagon to walk toward the person who is in the wrong until there are only ten paces between them. When this is done, Amredat pronounces judgment."

"Indeed this is interesting," remarked Khiddon. "And this is exactly how it will take place tonight?"

"As I have described it," the shopkeeper assured him.

Khiddon's face wrinkled in a show of confusion. "How can that be?" he wondered. "Will not Amredat be one of the two persons on trial? Either he is right or Shabbal is right. Or am I wrong?"

Samson, watching the scene, could hardly keep from laughing at the sight of the shopkeeper's amazement. His jaw dropped, and into his eyes came a startled look not unmixed with fright. "You are right!" he exclaimed hoarsely. "The trial will *have* to be between Amredat and his nephew!"

Khiddon nodded sagely. "Of course. And I hope that Walking Dagon knows it, for if it walks toward Amredat—"

The shopkeeper gasped. "Impossible!" he exclaimed.

"Why impossible?" asked Khiddon calmly. "Suppose Walking Dagon thinks that Shabbal is right and Amredat is wrong, will he not walk toward Amredat?"

All at once the shopkeeper became busy with his wares. "You talk too much and none too wisely, stranger," he growled. "I have wasted enough time on you." He turned his back and went to the rear of the store.

"Come, my good man," Khiddon called after him. "I am asking you only because others may ask me. Here, sell me some of your wares." He pointed to a shelf laden with clay tablets. "Two of those, please, and a writing stick."

Khiddon paid for his purchase and the two turned away from the shop.

"Why the tablets?" asked Samson.

"This statue of Dagon interests me greatly," Khiddon

replied. "I suggest we pay a visit to this wondrous idol."

Samson gave his companion a quick glance. "You mean—right in Reshak's own garden?" he asked.

"In Reshak's own garden, of course," Khiddon declared. "I do not promise that Reshak will invite us to inspect it, but there are other ways."

"The tablets?" guessed Samson.

Khiddon winked broadly. "You shall soon see," he said. "Come."

They found Reshak's residence without difficulty. It was next to the palace—a large house of rough stone, surrounded by a high wall and ringed with lofty palm trees. On either side of the iron gate the figure of Dagon, half-man, half-fish, was imbedded in the wall.

"This is not the Dagon we are looking for," Khiddon remarked. "If either of these walks he will have to take the wall along with him."

A solitary guard was on duty on the other side of the gate.

"I should like to see Reshak, the High Priest of Ashdod—at once," Khiddon haughtily addressed the guard, before the latter could utter a word.

"Away with you," the guard answered. "You have no business here. Even if my master were here he would not be interested in seeing anyone like you."

"So!" Khiddon's voice shook with anger; inwardly he felt elated that Reshak was not about. "You dare be the judge as to whether I have business here or not? It is bad enough that Reshak himself is not here to greet me, the foremost artist in Philistia! Very well! Many a season will change before I come again. And should Reshak ask me the reason, I shall tell him: 'The sentry at your gate refused to let me enter.'" With this, Khiddon turned about.

"Wait—wait there," the guard called. The "artist" appeared harmless enough, and Reshak did not like his servants to make any mistakes. He opened the gate slightly. "What about him?" he asked, pointing to Samson.

"My tablet-bearer?" asked Khiddon in a shocked tone. "Do you think that I, the foremost artist in the land, would carry those heavy tablets myself?"

The guard hastily opened the gate wide. "Come in, then," he said.

Samson could hardly restrain himself from laughing as Khiddon strode past the gate with the air of a conquering hero back from the wars. "Lead us to Walking Dagon," he ordered.

The guard hastily opened the gate wide. "Come in." He pointed to a wide path on the left. "It is in the garden, over there," he directed. "I cannot leave the gate."

The figure of Walking Dagon was set on a square wooden platform, slightly less than a man's height above the ground. The platform itself stood on four wooden legs, hidden from sight by a heavy sea-green drape wrapped around the base from the ground to the top of the platform, so that Dagon appeared to be resting on a block of solid green. At each corner of the platform was an iron ring; these, guessed the riddle-master, were for the poles by which the statue was carried about.

Khiddon came to a halt a few feet from the statue. "One tablet, boy," he commanded loudly, stretching his left hand toward Samson.

"Yes, sir," responded Samson. "Here it is, sir." He handed a tablet to "the foremost artist in Philistia," but the latter was in no hurry to do anything with it. He backed away a few paces, cocking his head first to one side then to the other, until he had a clear view of the path leading to the gate. The guard was there, leaning on his spear.

Khiddon came back to the statue. "We are now in the kettle, Samson," he whispered. "Let us hope that the soup does not get scorched."

"What if someone comes upon us here?" asked Samson.

"Ah, do not worry," Khiddon reassured him. "I have had some experience with engraving in clay, since riddle-mastery is not always rewarding. I trust that my skill has not deserted me." With this, he began cutting into the tablet, using short, swift strokes to outline the figure of Walking Dagon.

Samson heard Khiddon whistle softly. Where the idol's fishtail fanned out to the platform, a row of holes, each no bigger than a coin, had been bored into the wood. There were similar holes high on Dagon's chest, half-hidden beneath the square wooden beard that adorned its chin.

Suddenly Samson's eye caught sight of a figure, draped in a cloak of red and silver, hurrying down the path. Khiddon also had seen the newcomer but he kept on cutting into the tablet. "It must be Reshak," he murmured, without moving his lips. "Be calm."

The face of Ashdod's High Priest was twisted with anger. "What are you two doing here?" he demanded.

"Ah, Your Excellency!" exclaimed Khiddon, turning toward Reshak with a deep bow. "It is indeed a happy moment for me, that you have come just as I am recording on clay the far-famed figure of Walking Dagon."

Reshak flung out his hand. "Give it to me," he ordered.

Khiddon, with a bow even lower than the first, handed the tablet to Reshak. Watching closely, he saw the look on the High Priest's face change from anger to surprise. The engraving on the tablet was quite good, and below the figure Khiddon had thoughtfully added, at the last moment: WALKING DAGON OF RESHAK, NOBLE HIGH PRIEST OF ASHDOD.

"So!" exclaimed Reshak, and there was no mistaking the pleasant note in his voice. "And what are you planning to do with this?"

Once more Khiddon bowed. "This tablet I shall offer to Your Excellency, a gift from a poor artist to the foremost dignitary of Philistia. On the second tablet I shall create a similar image, to show to others for a small price."

Reshak suddenly became impatient. "Keep your tablet, my good artist," he cried. "Here is something for your work, and be gone with you." He tossed a coin toward Khiddon.

"Ah, Your Excellency," exclaimed the "artist" with an injured air, yet deftly catching the coin. "If my work does not please you, then never shall I touch another tablet."

"Enough, enough, be gone!" commanded Reshak. He followed the two until they were on the other side of the gate, then hurried into the house.

"Now that," observed Khiddon, "was a narrow escape. But at least we know the secret of Walking Dagon."

"The holes in the statue?" ventured Samson.

"Exactly. I looked through one hole and saw light on the other side, which means that the statue is hollow. The holes near the base are to look through from inside the idol, while those at the chest are for breathing. Yes, Dagon walks because someone carries him."

Samson's eyes opened wide. "How can that be?" he wondered. "The shopkeeper told us that Amredat allows people to examine the statue."

"Oh, that?" laughed Khiddon. "It is a simple matter indeed. Except when Dagon 'walks,' whoever carries him remains up inside the idol. He is already there when the priests pick Dagon up in Reshak's garden for the trip to the sporting field. When the statue is set down he lowers himself to the ground, probably through a trapdoor in the platform, lifts up the idol and proceeds to walk— exactly in the direction that Reshak and Amredat had already decided that he should."

"And then?"

"My guess," continued Khiddon, "is that, as soon as the verdict is given by Amredat, the carrier climbs back into the statue, draws the trapdoor up after himself and rests from his labors, while the priests carry Walking Dagon back to Reshak's garden. When it is safe he crawls out. That, I think, is the story."

Samson shook his head. "Your words ring with reason," he admitted, "but what does it have to do with us, now that we do know the secret of Walking Dagon?"

Khiddon did not answer immediately. He let his eyes rest on the city of Ashdod.

"I do not know, Samson," he said finally. "Do not forget that we are here in Philistia because you have a mission. Once you have reached manhood, it will be your task to deliver your people from Philistine hands. By that time, the lot of your tribe will be worse, not better, for tyranny becomes more cruel with each passing year."

Samson nodded gravely.

"The wicked become stronger," continued Khiddon. "Unless their course of oppression is checked, the weak become even weaker."

"But what does this have to do with Walking Dagon?" Samson wanted to know.

"A great deal," the riddle-master replied tersely. "If you can do something, now, to sow confusion among the Philistines, you may succeed in weakening them for the future. That is why, tonight, Dagon must be made to walk toward the last person on earth that the Ashdodians would expect him to walk."

"Toward Amredat?"

"Indeed, toward Amredat himself. It should not be difficult. We shall find out what the priests wear for this occasion, and tonight you will be one of them. The crowds will be pressing about the procession, so that your presence will not be noticed as you mingle with the bearers of the statue. When the idol is set down you will have to worm your way inside the drape immediately, before Betan has time to climb down."

"You are sure that it is Betan who will be there?" asked Samson.

"I am," replied Khiddon, "if what we have been told is true. But it makes little difference. The important thing is for you to act quickly. Betan must not be allowed to climb out of the statue. Even if you overcome him you will either have to leave him on the ground, where he will be seen as soon as the statue moves off, or push his limp body back up into the idol, which you will find almost impossible."

Samson nodded. "I understand," he replied quickly. "I must get under the platform before the priests come to a halt, then place my hand under the trapdoor and keep Betan from opening it."

"That is right," said Khiddon approvingly. "I am sure that the trapdoor opens outwardly, otherwise Betan would find it difficult to get in or out. Now Betan will certainly try to break out of his prison, once he realizes that something has gone wrong, but if he has any sense at all he will remain quiet and hope for the best. Amredat would hardly be pleased if the trick of Walking Dagon is revealed in the presence of all Ashdod."

For a moment the long-haired boy was silent. "One problem still remains," he observed. "When I come to a stop in front of Amredat he is likely to become so angry that he might draw his sword and rush at me through the drape, thinking that Betan has betrayed him."

Khiddon sighed. "Yes, what you say is certainly possible. I therefore leave it to you, Samson, whether you wish to go through with this plan or not."

"Of course I do," laughed Samson. "It is not every day that I can be a Philistine priest, fight off Ashdod's strong man, and make Dagon walk."

AMREDAT BEGAN his preparations for the trial a short hour after sunset.

He had dined privately with Reshak that evening, and the two had gone over every detail of what was going to take place. Together they enjoyed several cups of wine, offering each cupful as a toast to Walking Dagon.

The idea of the hollow idol was Reshak's. He had noted that Amredat's strong hand in ruling Ashdod was arousing some resentment among the people. Members of the city's most prominent families were beginning to speak out against the means he was using to increase his own wealth and power. If Amredat could show that Dagon was on his side, so reasoned Reshak, the opposition would be silenced.

Amredat was delighted with Reshak's plan. All the details fitted into place easily—until there came up the question of who should, or even could, carry Dagon about. Betan was finally selected, not only because he was the strongest man in Ashdod but also because his mind was the simplest; he could be trusted to obey orders without understanding them in the least.

There remained the matter of the hollow figure of Walking Dagon. How could that be kept a secret? Amredat had a ready solution. All the necessary materials were assembled in a hidden room beneath the palace. Ashdod's finest wood-carver was summoned, and he remained in the room until the work was completed. On his way home, with five pieces of gold as the reward for his labors, he was attacked by "robbers" and killed. The secret of Walking Dagon was safe.

On the next day a strange story began making the

rounds of the city. Amredat, so went the story, had fallen asleep while pondering an important case that was coming up for trial, and dreamt a dream. In his dream he called upon Dagon to help him make the right decision, and Dagon told him that if he would go to Reshak's garden someone would guide him to the home of the guilty person. Amredat awoke and immediately went to see Reshak for an interpretation of the dream, when lo and behold! At the gate stood Reshak's statue of the idol, and, as Amredat came near, it moved away from the gate and headed down one of the streets, to the home of Maredo, a well-known citizen of Ashdod who had once owned a large tract of land which now belonged to Amredat. It so happened that he was also one of the two men whose trial was taking place before the ruler of Ashdod.

But the story did not end there. Though no one was about when Amredat and the statue left Reshak's house, the entire household was awake when they returned, although it was barely dawn. Reshak, it seems, had been unable to sleep; something told him that the statue of Dagon was not in its usual place in the garden. When he discovered this to be true he aroused his servants and all the priests, so that the miracle of Walking Dagon was witnessed by enough people to spread the story from one end of Philistia to the other.

Reshak then issued an official statement, proclaiming Ashdod to have been chosen for this honor because its people were faithful to Dagon. But Amredat insisted that Walking Dagon, as the statue was now called, be put to test. Another important trial was scheduled to take place a week later. The ruler of Ashdod ordered the trial to be held at the sporting field, where each and every citizen of the city might watch and judge for himself.

The elders of Ashdod were loud in their praise of Amredat and his wise decision. They also appointed Reshak to arrange the details of the unusual event.

On the night of the trial all Ashdod was to be found at the sporting field. Along the edge of the circular arena itself, where began the round slope on which the onlookers sat, Reshak's servants, using white stone ground into powder, marked out a broad ring, which none but those who were to take part in the ceremony could enter. All around along this ring blazing torches turned the night into day.

It was a most impressive sight, as indeed Reshak had planned it to be. First to enter the ring was Amredat himself, in full warrior dress and escorted by a troop of palace guards. He ascended a small platform at the edge of the arena and remained there, standing with arms folded across his chest. At this point the two persons whose case was to be tried that night came into the ring and paused at its center. There they were joined by Reshak and heard his warning that the verdict of Walking Dagon was to be respected and obeyed, under pain of death.

With this, Reshak joined Amredat on the platform, while the two men took their places at opposite ends across the circle. Then the quiet of the night was shattered by shrill blasts of horns mingled with blood-curdling shrieks, as the priests burst into the circle, twisting about in their hooded cloaks like deadwood before a gale. They made a turn of the arena in this fashion and reached their starting point in time to escort Walking Dagon to its place in the center of the field, carried there by twelve of their number on poles thrust through the rings in the platform.

Slowly Reshak read the full details of the trial. Then, making sure that Walking Dagon was alone in the field, he called on the idol to render true judgment by walking toward the person in the wrong.

The statue rose slightly until the bottom of the drape was half a hand's breadth above the ground. It rocked slightly from side to side, then straightened itself and headed directly toward one of the men, stopping some ten paces away from him.

All this took place in dead silence. The Ashdodians sat frozen to the rough grass on the slope of the sporting field, hardly believing their eyes. Here and there a whisper of disbelief was heard. Was there a trick to Walking Dagon? But Amredat was prepared for the doubters. Even before the two men in the trial were brought before him to hear the verdict, the ruler of Ashdod called on the elders to inspect Walking Dagon. The elders looked inside the drape and found nothing under the platform. Dagon had indeed walked all by himself.

What still remained to the trial now passed quickly. As soon as the verdict was announced, the priests carrying the statue came forth with their poles and bore Walking Dagon out from the field, barely managing to move at all with the throng milling about them. The first judgment by Walking Dagon had ended.

More such trials followed—not many and not too often. Even so, the crowds at these trials became smaller and smaller, although the judgment of Walking Dagon was never questioned. In time more people came to see the wrestling matches than to witness the miracle.

But never before was there so much excitement as on the night that Walking Dagon was to decide between Shabbal and his uncle, Amredat the ruler of Ashdod.

Hours before the appointed hour the slope surrounding the arena was thick with people. They jostled and pushed each other to get as close as possible to the circle of white dust. The slaves holding the torches had to summon the guards to keep from being forced into the circle by the throng pressing hard behind them.

During the other trials the townspeople had gone into wagering, not only on the outcome but also on the number of steps that Walking Dagon would make, the colors in Reshak's costume (which he changed from one trial to another), and other items which made attendance at the trial more interesting. It was the same this time. But one item had no takers; no one was willing to wager that the statue would walk toward Amredat.

Khiddon, standing near the entrance to the sporting field, heard the wagers being made all around him, and he sighed deeply. There he was, the only one in Ashdod who knew which way Dagon would walk, yet to wager on it was far too dangerous. Again Khiddon sighed at the fortune that was slipping away.

He sat down to await the ceremony. In his mind he went over every detail of the plan which he had worked out with Samson. The hooded cloak was not easy to get, but Khiddon managed to find one in a shop where most of the priests did their trading; he was taking it, he told the shopkeeper, back across the Jordan, to show the priests there what their brethren in Ashdod were wearing. Decked out in his new attire, Samson was to slip into the ranks of the priests on their way to the field. In the darkness, and with spectators lining the route, this could easily be done. But from that point on Samson would be on his own.

At exactly midway in the elaborate rite the blare of horns announced the arrival of Ashdod's ruler. Every eye was upon him as he strode, in full warrior dress, to his place on the platform. He stood there for a moment, amidst a silence so deep that the cry of a jackal in the distance sounded like a lion's roar.

Slowly, piece by piece, he allowed his armor to clatter to the platform. From his arms he removed the jingling golden bands. These he handed to one servant, while another slipped over his shoulders the cloak of coarse gray linen that the persons on trial wore for the occasion. This done, Amredat stepped down from the platform and walked to the center of the circle.

Much to Amredat's satisfaction, this move impressed the throng exactly as Reshak had said it would. For when Shabbal entered the arena, a moment later, not a sound came from the crowd, not a single cheer from those who called Shabbal their hero and champion. Khiddon, huddled a few steps away from the young man, saw his lips tighten in a grim line, as he walked with a firm step to the center of the ring—and his uncle.

Reshak now entered the arena, and there was no need for trumpets to announce his arrival. His vestments brought a gasp from the crowd. His cloak was of bright green, embroidered with silver-painted shells. Around his waist was a sash of pure white, to which an apron of silvery scales was attached. His head was adorned with a red velvet turban fringed with gold coins. In his hand he carried a crooked staff, fashioned out of driftwood but polished to a high luster.

The High Priest approached the two men at the center of the arena. With his staff he drew a circle about them in the earth and, gathering some soil at the staff's tip, smeared it on their gray cloaks.

"As the earth lives forever and witnesses the deeds of men," he proclaimed, "so shall it witness the deeds of them that stand in judgment. As the circle never begins and never ends, so shall the judgment of Walking Dagon never cease, and woe to him who disregards his judgment, for his days shall be as black as the bottom of the sea on days of storm, and in the eyes of men he will be as naught."

With this, Reshak turned about and went to the platform. There he raised his staff and brought it down on the wood, three times.

As in echo came the procession of Walking Dagon. It began with a long, loud outcry on the part of the hooded priests; accustomed as the Ashdodians were to this wild howl, it still sent a shudder through them. The priests came in two lines, flanking the statue and its bearers, but as soon as Walking Dagon was well inside the arena the lines broke, and the priests began swirling and twisting all the way to the center of the field, and at the same time keeping up the loud chant without letup.

Khiddon strained his eyes to catch some glimpse of Samson among the priests, but he could see nothing of the boy. This meant that Samson had managed to get in under the platform of the statue before it reached the arena. Of course, there was the chance that Samson could not get to Walking Dagon at all ... The riddle-master leaned back and waited.

On the platform where Reshak was standing, two Nubian slaves now came up with a huge gong. Once, twice crashed the gong and the priests immediately fell silent. It took them but a moment to withdraw from the arena, leaving the glistening figure of Walking Dagon alone in the enclosure.

It was now Reshak's turn to read the facts of the trial. Knowing that he would, this time, have to pronounce the verdict as well, the High Priest of Ashdod had prepared himself very carefully. To have his voice at its best he had kept away from the well-salted fish, his favorite delicacy.

He had written down the facts of the trial and the verdict on one scroll. Amredat himself had dictated the verdict: Shabbal was to be stripped of all his possessions, which were to go to his uncle, and would be banished forever from Ashdod. Neither Reshak nor Amredat considered it necessary to think of any other outcome of the trial.

Reshak advanced to the edge of the platform and majestically opened the scroll. His voice carried to the outermost rim of the circle:

"In the name of mighty Dagon, ruler of the sea and all that is therein, guardian of Philistia and victor over its enemies, we have in our midst, to stand before him in righteous judgment, two citizens of Ashdod, each seeking guidance in the path of truth."

This was how Reshak began his recitation at all of the trials, and the throng waited impatiently for more.

The High Priest adjusted the scroll and continued:

"Says Shabbal that his soul cries out for the poor and the oppressed; that his heart can find no peace; that his tongue must speak out for the hurt and the suffering, until the day will come that the poor will all be blessed with wealth. Then he will cry out no more, but will pray for the well-being of the city and its ruler."

A low murmur passed through the throng. Reshak's statement of Shabbal's case was very fine indeed. To none in the crowd did it occur that Amredat, being sure which way Dagon would walk, felt that it would not hurt him to be generous toward his nephew.

Reshak went on:

"Says Amredat that everywhere there are rich and there are poor; that if the poor become wealthy, the wealthy will have to become poor; that whoever seeks to change this order is a threat to the peace and happiness of all. As ruler of Ashdod he therefore asks that his nephew, the young Shabbal, whom he loves dearly, be made to cease speaking folly and breeding disorder."

The mention of Amredat's love for his nephew brought a titter from the crowd, but it quickly died down as Reshak again took to the scroll:

"To you, O Dagon, do I, Reshak the High Priest of Ashdod, now turn, and I plead that you direct your steps toward him who is in the wrong and stand not more than ten paces before him. Answer me, O Dagon, as you have in the past. Answer me, in the sight and in the hearing of all here assembled, so that your name and fame be forever enshrined in the hearts of all true Philistines. Answer me, O Dagon!"

All eyes now turned to the center of the arena. One moment passed, then another, and the statue began to stir.

Amredat, watching intently, saw immediately that Walking Dagon was acting in a rather unusual fashion. The statue rose a bit from the ground in one steady move, not in its customary wobbly fashion. Then, instead of proceeding toward one or the other of the men on trial, it began dancing about in a small circle.

"That Betan!" muttered Amredat to himself. "He knows that the eyes of the city are upon him. Even though none can see his feat, he still must show it."

Now Walking Dagon decided that he had danced enough. The statue set off in a straight course, but directly toward Reshak!

Amredat was now boiling inside. Betan must have taken a few overly generous gulps of strong drink, despite the repeated warnings that he was to stay sober on trial nights!

As though realizing its mistake the statue stopped suddenly and turned back. Again the desire to frolic must have seized it, for it now took up its dance—forward, backward, sideways . . .

Now it was Reshak's turn to fume with rage. How did Betan dare to make sport with Dagon, in full sight of the people! In his mind the High Priest began fashioning a few devices to punish the offender—after the conclusion of the trial.

Walking Dagon at last decided to behave as befitted the occasion. He returned to the exact center of the arena, faced Shabbal and slowly began to advance toward the young man.

Amredat breathed more easily now. Betan had finally come to his senses. Still, the strong one would have to receive some sort of punishment for his silly antics.

With every step that Walking Dagon took, the murmur of the crowd, which had been on the light side, deepened into a growl. Then, some twenty paces from Shabbal, the statue came to a halt.

Both Reshak and Amredat guessed that Betan had paused for breath, but the crowd, not expecting Walking Dagon to tire, was now completely bewildered. Its confusion grew even more when the statue abruptly turned around and went back to its starting point.

It didn't stop there. With increasing speed and unmistakable firmness it moved in the opposite direction, straight toward Amredat. As the latter's eyes opened in horror, Walking Dagon came down with a thud, ten paces in front of the ruler of Ashdod!

The stunned silence of the crowd broke, like a thunder-clap, into a mighty roar. Everyone was on his feet, and in the excitement there was a surge forward. The torches in the hands of the slaves swayed like trees in a gale.

In all this tumult Reshak saw something that caused him to leave the platform in a hurry. Amredat had seized a short sword from one of the guards and was now striding toward the statue. There was no mistaking his purpose.

"No, no," hissed Reshak, catching hold of Amredat's arm. "Keep away, or all will be lost."

Amredat's face was twisted with black rage, but the arm with the sword dropped to his side. "That Betan," he cursed. "I shall have his hands and feet cut off!"

"Go back," urged Reshak. "I shall pronounce the verdict. You have nothing to fear."

Calm returned again to the sporting field as the High Priest mounted the platform. Reshak did some quick thinking. Walking Dagon had put Amredat in a bad position. Shabbal was the winner in the trial, and the verdict had to show it that way. Still, as long as the people of Ashdod did not know the secret of the statue, the situation was not desperate. There was Betan, of course, but with his tongue cut out he would be no threat. Reshak motioned to the Nubians to strike the gong.

"Walking Dagon decrees," he proclaimed to the hushed audience, "that Shabbal, being sincere of purpose and of pure heart, is to have freedom to speak as he wishes on behalf of the poor."

A weak cheer greeted the announcement. Above it rose an angry blur of words, among which "taxes" was easily the loudest.

Reshak moistened his lips and glanced at Amredat. The ruler of Ashdod was staring at the ground. Once more the High Priest ordered the gong to be struck. "And for the period of one year," he went on, "those who declare themselves to be poor shall not have to pay taxes."

This time there were widespread cries of approval. Many in the crowd spilled over into the arena, and, before the guards could stop them, they all but upset the statue of Dagon with their embraces. In the confusion no one saw a figure crawl out from beneath Dagon.

It was long past midnight. The sporting field lay deserted in the moonlit stillness. Even the acrid smell of the torches, the last bit of evidence of what had taken place there earlier, had given way before the fresh breeze from the west.

Khiddon and Samson met each other, as they had planned, at the entrance to the inn near the city gates. They found it crowded with people; the excitement of the evening made sleep unthinkable.

Huge bowls of hot fish broth were on the table in the center of the dining hall, along with bread fried in olive oil. This was Ashdod's favorite snack. Khiddon and his companion filled their earthen dishes with the broth, took a handful of the fried bread and went out to the courtyard, where long rows of wooden benches had been set out against the wall that enclosed the inn. They found a quiet corner where they were all by themselves.

"No, I surely do not envy Betan," Khiddon remarked. "Since he himself does not know exactly what had happened, he will find it most difficult to explain it to others."

"He might have escaped on the way back to the field," suggested Samson.

"Perhaps," replied Khiddon, "although I doubt it. More likely, he thought that Dagon himself had imprisoned him, in punishment for all the 'trials' which he had helped Amredat to conduct. How hard *did* he try to get out?"

Samson chuckled. "Like a wild boar. At first he stamped with his foot on the trapdoor. If it were not for my thick hair I would be walking about with a sore skull for weeks."

Khiddon put his plate aside. "For a moment," he

confessed, "as I saw you dancing about with the statue, I was worried that you could not see where you were going. Betan would have used the holes in the base of the idol, but these were above the trapdoor. What did you do?"

Samson shook his head. "I saw this problem as soon as I had slipped inside the drape in the course of the procession. It was pitch black. I had to keep my fingertips on both sides of the drape in order to go along in the same direction with the statue. What I did then was to tear a hole in the front wall of the drape, on a level with my eyes, like a little window."

"Good," approved Khiddon. "It will be some time before Amredat and Reshak will recover from tonight's performance by Walking Dagon. It may even be that Ashdod has seen the last of these trials."

"Why do you think so?" asked Samson.

"For two reasons," replied the riddle-master. "If Betan did get away before the statue returned to Reshak's garden, Amredat will be too busy hunting him down to prevent the secret from becoming known. For a man of Betan's size it will not be easy to hide, and I am sure that Amredat will find him. Even so, however, I doubt whether Amredat and Reshak would be willing to have someone carry on in Betan's place; Betan's 'treachery' could be repeated."

Samson was still not satisfied. "But what if Betan did not try to escape?" he asked. "He might wait and tell Amredat that someone else had carried the statue, with himself inside it."

Khiddon laughed lightly. "I do not think so," he replied. "It will never enter Betan's mind that there exists anyone on this earth capable of performing such a feat of strength.''

A strange noise coming from the dining hall broke into Khiddon's words. One of the townsmen had come into the room, and his appearance immediately brought a cluster of eager people about him. Khiddon and Samson rose and edged toward the doorway.

"You *must* be the bearer of some kind of tidings, Rokhil,'' the innkeeper cried. "Speak out, and we shall listen.''

Rokhil was still gasping for breath. "It is Amredat and Reshak and Betan and Walking Dagon!'' he exclaimed, pointing to the bowls on the table.

The others waited impatiently while Rokhil gulped down the spicy broth. "What about them, Rokhil?'' demanded the innkeeper, as the others came even closer.

"Betan is dead!''

The innkeeper grasped Rokhil's arm. "The whole story,'' he demanded, "and a goatskin of wine will be yours.''

Rokhil was so anxious to tell the whole story that he paid little attention to the innkeeper's offer. "From the sporting field,'' he began, "I followed Walking Dagon to Reshak's house. My brother was one of the priests in the procession, and I wanted to have a word with him.''

"About the outcome of the trial?'' someone asked eagerly.

"No, not about the trial,'' retorted Rokhil, much annoyed by the interruption. "It was about a family matter which concerns no one here. Now,'' he continued, "when I came to the gate I found that Reshak had ordered that everyone be kept outside, even the priests."

"But the priests live in Reshak's house," exclaimed the innkeeper.

"True, true," replied Rokhil, "but I am telling you that this time Reshak ordered everyone to remain on the other side of the gate. The priests who had taken Walking Dagon back to the garden also had to leave the grounds."

"And Betan?" asked the innkeeper. "What did he have to do with all this? Did he tear down the gates?"

Rokhil stared at the speaker. "Tidings you want, and foolish questions you ask. Let me speak."

Cries of approval came from all sides, and the innkeeper drew back.

"You ask about Betan," went on Rokhil. "Let me first tell you what I did, for as you know I cannot rest when there is something to be learned."

Light laughter swept the room. Even the old women in Ashdod admitted that Rokhil was more than their match when it came to gathering gossip and news.

"I slipped away," continued Rokhil, lowering his voice, "and I climbed up a tree overlooking Reshak's garden—at the risk of my life, you understand. Then, looking down, I beheld Walking Dagon, lying on his back. The drape around the base had been torn away, and Reshak and Amredat were both kneeling there on the ground and pulling at something which I could not make out, at first."

The room was now as silent as a tomb. "By this time," Rokhil went on, "I was shaking like a leaf. Luckily it was not a tree laden with fruit which I had climbed, for every single one would have come down." His voice dropped even lower. "At last I could see what it was that they had been pulling. I could see it was Betan. I could also see that he was dead. His face was blue, even in the light of the torches."

In the courtyard Khiddon and Samson looked at each other. "Do you suppose they killed him?" the boy whispered.

"Hardly," returned Khiddon, "if what this fellow is telling is true Betan probably died of fright, either while you were carrying him or later."

Inside the inn Rokhil was waiting for the buzzing to die down. "I almost fell out of the tree," he declared. "Then, as Reshak and Amredat got up, I decided that it was time for me to come down, which I did, with my last remaining strength. When I got back to the gate I heard Reshak ordering everyone to be let in and to go on to the garden."

Khiddon nudged his companion. "I think I know what is coming," he murmured.

"We all gathered about Reshak and Amredat and Betan and Walking Dagon," Rokhil said. "Reshak then told us that Betan had tried to learn the secret of Walking Dagon and had been stricken dead for it. And indeed, looking at Betan's blue face, anyone could see that he had died an unnatural death — a most fitting punishment, I must say!"

Again Khiddon nudged Samson. Yes, Reshak was a clever one!

The men in the dining hall remained stunned. Betan! He was not known to be curious about gods and such. "What then?" pleaded the innkeeper, as Rokhil appeared to have come to the end of his narrative.

"Then," returned Rokhil slowly, "Reshak took one of the torches and held it to the drape. It caught fire, then the wooden platform, then Walking Dagon. When all that was left was a heap of ashes, Reshak took a handful and sprinkled it over Betan's body. This, he said, was the only way to avert Dagon's anger from Ashdod. Tomorrow it will be announced in the market place that Dagon will walk no more."

Under his breath the innkeeper muttered a string of curses. Walking Dagon trials had brought many visitors to Ashdod, and his own inn had reaped much profit. But if Reshak had so decreed, so it would have to be.

The dining hall began to empty, and soon the innkeeper was alone in the room, clearing away the scraps from the table.

Samson followed his companion to the dark corridor that led into the interior of the inn. "I still cannot believe all that has happened," he whispered. "This day has been like a strange dream."

"No, not so strange, Samson," replied Khiddon. "Amredat and Reshak fashioned Walking Dagon to serve their own ends. When the idol could be of no more use they destroyed it. So it is with all the idols of the Philistine and the Canaanites and the others; like any other tools, when their usefulness is over, out they go."

They reached the end of the corridor and turned into the sleeping chamber. About them others were deep in slumber for the night, while above Reshak's garden the moonlight shone on a scattered heap of ashes.

The Bandits of Kupta

THE RAIN was still falling steadily, pelting the overcast countryside with cold windblown drops, when Khiddon and Samson came in sight of Nappa, "village of the blacksmiths," a few hundred paces off the main highway to Gath. Already the air was thick with the smoke of the furnaces, and the clanging of hammer on anvil beat down on the ears of the travelers.

The weather was good enough when the two had started out, but experience had taught them to take along capes of skilfully woven palm leaves, used to keep off the water of the winter rains. These were now falling apart. Khiddon and his companion decided that the noise of the anvils could not be as bad as the drenching downpour. They guided their mules into the road that led to Nappa.

All the houses in the village were made of mud and stone; tents were not safe where sparks kept flying from the glowing forges. Only here and there, far beyond the village, a few shepherds' tents glistened in the rain.

A dog's bark greeted the travelers. They dismounted at what appeared to be the village inn and went in through the doorway. In the small, square room there was not a soul to be seen.

"It has been raining so hard that wayfarers are not being expected," remarked Khiddon in disgust. He nodded toward a door at the rear of the room. "See if you can find someone, Samson," he pleaded. "I know not of which I shall die first: of hunger or of weariness."

Before Samson could take a step, the door opened and a small boy entered. Khiddon at once showed signs of life.

"Ah, there, my fine lad," he exclaimed. "You are the son of the proprietor? Pray fetch your father hither, so that he may serve us food and drink."

"My father," replied the boy, "is a blacksmith."

Khiddon sighed. "My teeth are too old for iron," he muttered. "Can you fetch the owner of this inn, perhaps?"

The boy eyed the riddle-master. "What is your name?" he asked.

Khiddon passed his hand over his eyes; the boy was obviously neither hungry nor tired, and he could stand there and ask questions all day. "Come here, my lad," he finally said.

The boy moved closer, but not too near.

"You are a clever one, I am sure," Khiddon went on in his most soothing tones. "Now, when the innkeeper gets here he, too, will want to know my name. When I give it to him, you will also hear it. Therefore, go fetch the innkeeper, eh?"

The clever lad appeared to understand not a word, and the riddle-master was about to give up when a short, thick-set man entered the room.

"Ah, the proprietor of the establishment," cried Khiddon, rising from his seat. "If you will kindly give us food and drink we shall pay for it handsomely."

The innkeeper gave Khiddon and Samson a quick

look, then pointed to a small table in the corner of the room. With this, herding the little boy before him, he disappeared through the door.

Khiddon passed his palm over the surface of the table. It came away smeared with soot.

"What misfortune," he lamented. "Were it not for the rain we would be dining in Gath, without this miserable dirt to spice our food."

Samson bent down and blew hard at the table, and instantly the black dust rose like a cloud. "It is strange," he remarked. "Either the soot spreads quickly in this village, or no one has sat at this table for a long time."

The innkeeper came into the room, balancing slabs of bread and cheese in one hand and an earthen jug in the other. He had hardly reached the table when there came the noise of hoofbeats splashing along the rain-soaked roadway. The innkeeper hurriedly set down the food and rushed out.

Khiddon shrugged. "We pay for the food, not for the manner it is served," he said. "Let us therefore revive our hearts."

The two were so famished that several moments passed before they became aware that the clanging in the smithies had stopped. In its place came a faint rattling sound, as though a flock of iron birds were passing overhead.

"Something must be afoot," exclaimed Khiddon. He took a last sip of milk from the pitcher and rose to his feet. "Let us go."

Up the road, where stood the circle of Nappa's famed smithies, men were feverishly scurrying about in the drizzle. Their arms were laden with objects that Khiddon and Samson could not make out.

"They appear to be frightened," the riddle-master observed. "The horseman we heard before must have brought evil tidings."

"Perhaps we should leave," suggested Samson. "We may not be wanted."

"This we shall soon find out," Khiddon responded. "We shall walk toward them. Yet it is better that we do not speak first, since men who are frightened by one thing are suspicious of others."

All at once, from one of the blackened smithies in the circle, there came cries of anger—something about a "chariot" and "doorway." Khiddon and his companion edged closer to the smithy and peered in through the window opening.

Inside, surrounded by a knot of excited blacksmiths, stood the finest chariot that the travelers from Dan had ever seen. Its body, though sturdy in every detail, had been wrought with the rarest skill, from the rail at the top to the panels that curved in at the wheels at either side.

Several men had stationed themselves between the ironclad shafts of the chariots, but no move was being made to pull the vehicle out. Khiddon saw the reason at once. The doorway of the smithy was too narrow to let it come through!

Khiddon decided to change his plan of letting the villagers speak first. They had a problem on their hands, and the riddle-master knew that anything that would distract their attention from it would be welcome. He therefore stepped boldly into the smithy, with Samson right behind him.

"Any of you noble blacksmiths need a good apprentice?" Khiddon called out cheerfully.

The men in the smithy stared at the newcomers. One of them finally came forward. "I am Temun, the headman of Nappa," he said. "Where are you from, and what do you want?"

"From beyond the Jordan," Khiddon declared calmly, ignoring the cold stares about him. "It has reached our ears that the blacksmiths of Nappa are the finest between the Nile and the Euphrates. Therefore have I brought hither my nephew, who is blessed with much strength and is eager to learn the blacksmith's art." He turned to Samson. "Here, my dear nephew. Take hold of a sledge and show your prowess."

Samson looked about until his eye found a stack of hammers near the hearth. He picked up the heaviest and, wielding it with one hand as though it were a splinter of wood, he pounded it on the anvil with such force that sparks shot up to the ceiling.

The eyes of the bystanders opened wide.

"Have I deceived you?" demanded Khiddon. "Is not the strength of my nephew wondrous to behold? Let us therefore talk about his being with you here—"

Again the sound of hoofbeats came from the direction of the main highway. The men between the shafts dropped them to the ground and hurried out of the smithy. Temun remained inside, his eyes moving quickly from the chariot to the narrow doorway. All at once his shoulders sagged and he sighed heavily.

"Ah, something is wrong, O headman of Nappa,"

exclaimed Khiddon. "Perhaps I, the adviser of princes and the counsellor of chieftains, can be of help."

Temun looked at the riddle-master but in his eyes there was little hope. "Good advice is precious," he replied slowly, "but against Kupta it is of no avail."

"Kupta, Kupta," repeated Khiddon, as if striving to recall where he had heard the name. "Is Kupta a man or a beast of the field?"

Temun scowled. "Both, perhaps," he said. "You may not have heard the name beyond the Jordan. Here in Philistia the children sing songs about him."

"He is a hero, then?" ventured Khiddon.

"A hero?" scoffed Temun. "He is a hero, indeed! For does he not raid the territory of Dan and the Egyptian outposts? But he is also a bandit."

"Ah, a hero bandit," remarked Khiddon. "Or a bandit hero."

"A hero to the ignorant, a bandit to us who know him," Temun said sharply. "As a reward for his great deeds he comes and takes whatever he wants—food, clothing, finery. From us he takes the best of our wares—the swords and the spears and the ironware. To defend Philistia, he says. But we know better. After every visit of his we learn that he has sold our wares elsewhere. Now we hide our finest things, but we must still leave enough in the smithies, else he will destroy the village."

Khiddon shook his head in amazement. "And the rulers of the Philistine cities—have they nothing to say about this Kupta and his bandits?"

Temun snorted. "The rulers? Not one of them would harm a hair of Kupta's even though none would let him and his men live in the city. Most of his men are outcasts."

"This is very strange," commented Khiddon.

"Not at all," declared Temun. "All that a man convicted of some crime has to do to escape punishment is to declare that he wishes to join Kupta and fight against the enemies of our land. In this manner Kupta has been able to bring together a horde of outlaws whom no one dares challenge. They even built a walled city of their own, calling it by the name of their chieftain, so that none can disturb them or see how much loot they gathered."

Khiddon appeared to be lost in thought. "Do you mean to say," he said slowly, "that Kupta and his band could not find homes in any of the Philistine cities?"

Temun stared at the riddle-master. "It is true that no city would welcome them," he replied, "yet why should they want to live elsewhere? The walls of their own city are thick and strong and surrounded by a deep moat. Where else can they be as safe?"

"And now you think that Kupta is headed this way?"

"Without doubt. Kupta's city is but an hour's distance from here, and he always manages to visit us on his way home and to help himself to whatever he may find." Temun glanced at the chariot. "This I have fashioned for the ruler of Ashkelon. Now I shall have to tell him that Kupta is its owner—and all because we failed to measure the doorway."

"It can still be widened," suggested Khiddon.

"Oh, it will be widened," returned Temun grimly. "By Kupta and his men. They will not overlook such a prize."

Khiddon wanted to tell Temun that Samson could

pull the entire wall down in a twinkling, but it was too late. Hoofbeats mixed with the noise of rolling wheels announced the arrival of Kupta and his bandits. They came up the road like unruly guests heading for a feast.

Khiddon's mind worked quickly. "Does Kupta know you?" he asked Temun.

"Like his own brother," replied Temun. "I have pleaded with him often enough to spare us the work of our hands."

The riddle-master reached out toward the hearth and groped there for a moment with his fingers. They came away covered with soot, which he proceeded to smear on his face. "I am your helper," he said to Temun, "should Kupta come here."

Temun glanced at Samson. "What about the boy?"

"He will not be where Kupta can see him," Khiddon answered.

Temun hesitated, then turned toward the door. "I go to deal with Kupta," he said slowly. "If you can do something to keep him from despoiling us we shall reward you."

Khiddon waited until Temun had left, then hurried to the window opening, with Samson hard at his side. Kupta, they both guessed, was the broad, hairy-faced man at the head of the band, the one with the scar running halfway across his temple.

Samson gazed eagerly at the scene in front of the smithy. "I do not understand it," he whispered to Khiddon. "Surely the blacksmiths are strong enough to beat those bandits down."

"They are indeed," replied Khiddon. "Man to man they can crack the bandits' skulls. But this would only bring on the rest of the robbers. Besides, if Kupta's men are looked upon as heroes in Philistia, any attack on them would brand the blacksmiths as traitors. Kupta must be as clever as he is ugly."

The bandit chief finished looking over the villagers who had gathered by the smithies. There were neither women nor children in the small crowd.

"Ah, my dear Temun," exclaimed Kupta, as the headman of Nappa came slowly toward him. "It is indeed a rainy day but let there not be gloominess in your face. Do you really think that I have come to despoil your village? Ah, you are surprised to hear these words! But so have I heard, that you complain about my visits, claiming that I take away your wares. Yet it is to defend Philistia—and Nappa, to be sure—that my warriors and I use the arms that you fashion. Is it not so, Temun?"

The headman's eyes did not waver. "You also take tools and ornaments of iron," he replied. "Do you hurl *those* at the enemies of Philistia too?"

A guarded titter ran through the crowd. Much to Khiddon's surprise Kupta laughed heartily. "Temun, Temun," he chided. "Would you deny the defenders of Philistia a few ornaments with which to adorn their city? No, I shall not believe it of you." His tone changed. "And now my faithful men will gather *your* weapons with which *they* will defeat *your* enemies."

With cries of glee the bandits hurried into the smithies. At this, Khiddon whispered a few words into Samson's ear. When Kupta's men broke into the smithy they found Khiddon alone, working over the coals on the hearth. At the sight of the chariot the bandits stopped short, then, as one, they rushed back to their leader, each trying to get to him first with the news.

The bandit chieftain made no effort to conceal his delight. "Is she not a beauty!" he exclaimed, feasting his eyes on the chariot's trim lines. "Our dear Temun has truly excelled himself this time! How proud will he be to know that I shall make this chariot my very own, as I swoop down on the enemies of Philistia to destroy them! And wherever I drive this chariot, my dear Temun, I shall proclaim to all the wonders of your skill."

Temun's eyes flashed with scorn at this flowery speech but his voice was calm and even. "Indeed I shall be proud, O Kupta," he responded. "Yet I must tell you that this chariot my hands have fashioned for Salmidar, the ruler of Ashkelon. He, like all of us, is grateful to you for routing the enemies of Philistia. Why not then let me present the chariot to Salmidar and receive my reward first?"

Kupta grinned evilly. "Ah, my dear Temun," he retorted. "What you are suggesting is impossible! For if Salmidar gives me such a wonderful gift, then the rulers of the other cities will feel it their duty to do the same— and what would I do with five chariots?" He winked broadly at his men. "No, my dear Temun. I shall take this chariot, now, and drive it to my own city." With this, Kupta motioned to his men to wheel the chariot out of the smithy, but even before they could take hold of the shafts he noted that the doorway was too narrow. For some reason this struck him as being very funny. He threw back his head and laughed uproariously, unaware that Khiddon had come near Temun and was whispering into the headman's ear.

"Enough of this!" cried Kupta. He picked up a sledge and strode to the doorway. With a few well-placed blows that shook the squat building he widened the opening by two cubits, enough to let the chariot pass through with ease. This done, he threw the sledge aside and motioned to his men to go on with their task.

Four of the bandits took hold of the shafts and began pulling. The chariot did not budge.

"What is with you, weaklings?" shouted Kupta.

"It does not want to move," one of the four replied sheepishly.

Kupta threw him a withering glance. "Witless donkey!" he yelled. "Here, let me show you sons of donkeys how it is done."

The others made room for their chieftain. Kupta seized the shafts in both hands. "Together, pull!" he ordered.

The chariot remained motionless, as though imbedded in the earth.

Temun stepped forward. "I should have told you, O noble Kupta, why Salmidar ordered this chariot to be fashioned. It is because he intends to use it in the sacred processions honoring Dagon and the other gods of the sea. Perhaps it is Dagon himself who is causing the chariot to remain in its place. If so, O Kupta, I would not be surprised if Dagon were to cast his curse on anyone who tries to take it for himself, or even to move it."

The men holding the chariot let go of the shafts as though the iron enclosing the wood had suddenly turned red-hot. Only Kupta still held on to them.

Temun lost no time. "Go on, I pray you," he urged Kupta. "Take the chariot. If you can move it, then you are stronger than Dagon. But if you cannot, then surely Dagon will forgive neither you nor your men."

A harsh snarl came from Kupta's lips. He knew that he could not move the chariot. He could also see the look of panic on the face of his men. Some of them were even shaking with fright. It would not do, decided Kupta, that they show fear in front of the villagers.

"On our way," he shouted. "We fight the enemies of Philistia, not its gods. To your horses!"

Temun and the villagers watched the bandits ride out of Nappa, wagons rattling in the wake of the horses. With wide grins across their faces they returned to their smithies, and soon the pounding of hammers rose into the air.

Inside his own smithy Temun found Samson at Khiddon's side. The boy's knees were slightly red; this was the only evidence of what he had been doing.

The headman of Nappa was so choked with feelings of thanks that he could hardly speak, and Khiddon was the first to break the silence. "Now that your dear friend, the defender of Philistia, was good enough to knock out a wider passageway, you can wheel out the chariot without difficulty. Your people should be told that Dagon's spell had ended as soon as Kupta left the village."

Temun placed his hand on Khiddon's shoulder. "You are indeed our friend. You have rid us of Kupta forever. He will not have the nerve to show his face here again."

Khiddon shook his head. "I am afraid your lot may yet grow worse," he said. "Kupta will not let the matter rest. He has ways of finding out whether Salmidar had ordered the chariot for the processions, and when he learns the truth his vengeance will be a bitter one for you." He drew a deep breath and faced Temun squarely. "No, my friend; Kupta must be destroyed."

"But how?" asked Temun. "I have promised you a reward for what you have already done. You will receive far more if you remove this plague from us."

Again Khiddon shook his head. "My nephew and I seek no reward," he declared. "We are staying at the village inn. After the evening meal you will go there, and we shall speak out our thoughts."

The rain had stopped. Khiddon and Samson skirted the deep puddles in the road and made their way to the inn.

"I do not think that you found it too difficult to hold back the chariot, did you?" asked Khiddon.

"Not in the least," replied Samson. "I braced my knees against the ground and held fast, even though I was tempted to push the chariot forward and run over Kupta and his pack."

Khiddon nodded, grimly. "You will be doing more than running them down," he said, "if we are to remove the threat to Nappa—and to the tribe of Dan."

TEMUN CAME to the inn shortly after darkness had fallen. As he was about to enter, a figure detached itself from the shadows and took hold of his arm. It was Samson.

"My uncle is waiting for us a bit up the road," he whispered. "There are too many at the inn tonight."

"Celebrating Kupta's retreat, no doubt," smiled

Temun. "Let us go."

They found Khiddon pacing in a small circle, deep in thought.

"We could have spoken freely at the inn," the headman of Nappa remarked. "Every man in the village will be glad to have a hand in Kupta's downfall."

Khiddon laughed shortly. "A hand, yes, O Temun, but when one has a cup of strong drink before him the hand becomes weak and the tongue becomes diligent. I shall reveal my plan to you only, and when the time comes it will be your task to see that your people follow it. You will tell them what to do, but nothing more."

Temun was silent for a moment. "Whatever your plan may be, I shall see that it is carried out," he finally said.

"Let us go on with it, then," said Khiddon. "First, we must know more about Kupta's city. Tell us what you can about it."

The headman drew a deep breath. "The city—it is really a town in size, but because of its walls one calls it a city—lies between Gath and Timna, on a rise set in the midst of a plain, so that no one can approach it without being seen. Around the walls runs a deep moat, lined at the bottom with sharp stones and jagged bits of iron."

"Are there bridges across this moat?" asked Khiddon.

"Not bridges," stated Temun. "The walls have four gates, one for each direction. Whenever Kupta and his men go forth or come back, the gates are opened by those inside and heavy wooden planks are wheeled up to the moat and stretched across it."

Khiddon stroked his chin. "It would appear," he said slowly, "that an ordinary attack on the town is bound to fail." He pondered for a moment. "How many men does Kupta have?"

"Some two hundred," replied Temun, "but the number is always increasing. Outcasts from the cities immediately head for the town. Kupta takes them in, and once a month he makes a choice, whom to keep and whom to send away."

"Once a month?" wondered Khiddon.

"At the full of the moon," explained Temun. "On that night Kupta holds a grand feast, the noise of which can be heard throughout half of Philistia. There is eating and drinking and much sport."

"Very interesting," commented Khiddon. "The town must be fairly large, to have a sporting field."

Temun chuckled. "That is not the kind of sport that Kupta enjoys. The sport is furnished by these outcasts who want to become bandits. Kupta has each one perform some feat to show how brave he is, or how strong he is. If Kupta is satisfied with the performance, the lucky one stays. If not, Kupta orders the unlucky one pushed down into the moat, to make his way out of it as best as he can." He peered at Khiddon in the darkness. "What do you have in mind?" he asked.

Instead of replying, Khiddon bent down and picked up a pebble. With a quick motion he flipped it into the air. The pebble came down and struck Temun in the temple.

The headman of Nappa jumped aside. "What is this?" he cried angrily.

"Why," asked Kiddon calmly, "did you move away when the pebble hit you?"

Temun glowered at the riddle-master, but at once he

understood that there was some purpose to Khiddon's act. "If something strikes you, it is but natural to move aside, lest it strike you again."

"Excellent!" cried Khiddon. "Now tell me: if you would be standing here, but fenced in, and the pebbles would begin falling on you, what would you do?"

Temun laughed. "I would climb over the fence, or try to break it down, or, if I had to, burrow under it."

"That," said Khiddon slowly, "is how we shall cause defeat to visit Kupta."

"With a rain of pebbles?" scoffed Temun.

"Yes, with pebbles—of a sort," the riddle-master returned. "Now, how far off the road to Timna is the town?"

"A good thousand paces, if not more," replied Temun.

The reply did not seem to please Khiddon. "The distance is too short," he remarked.

"Too short for what?" Temun wanted to know.

"If what you say about Kupta's feasts is true," said Khiddon, "I am sure that the entire road near the town is crowded with spectators."

Temun stared at Khiddon in wonder. "Indeed you are right," he said. "So it was until two months ago. It happened that several outcasts who had been sent away by Kupta came to the Timna road. There the people jeered at them. This made the outcasts so angry that they attacked the people with their daggers. Quite a few were killed. Since then the road has been empty on those nights."

Khiddon grunted with satisfaction and glanced up

at the sky. The clouds had cleared away, and the bright rays of the moon shone over the countryside. "I judge that the moon will be full in three days," he said.

"In three days indeed," agreed Temun.

"Good." There was a new ring in Khiddon's voice, and Samson, knowing his companion well, felt that excitement lay ahead. "I believe," continued the riddle-master, "that there is a stone quarry about half a day's distance to the east. Tomorrow you will send men and two wagons to this quarry. They are to bring back stones, as much as the wagons will hold, each stone a cubit long, a cubit wide and a cubit thick. Should anyone ask why the stones, your men are to say that Nappa is building more smithies."

Temun nodded. "This will not be difficult to believe," he said, "for it is from this quarry that we obtained stones to build the smithies in our village."

"When the stones are here," continued Khiddon, "you and your men will split each stone into four, then load them back onto the wagons. On the third evening, when Kupta will be preparing for his feast, you are to drive these wagons toward Timna, so that they will reach the point nearest Kupta's town about midnight."

A puzzled look crossed Temun's face. "What will you be doing with these stones?" he wondered aloud.

"Stones?" repeated Khiddon quietly. "You mean pebbles—do you not, my dear Temun?"

THE MOON was well along its course across the cool autumn sky when Temun and the wagons reached their destination.

The headman of Nappa himself was not with his men. He had followed them from the village in his chariot. With him were Khiddon and Samson.

As Temun had said, there was no one on the Timna road, and none hailed the wagons as they creaked to a stop. Some fifteen men jumped to the ground and stood there, waiting.

"The moon is bright—almost too bright," Khiddon whispered to Samson after they had descended from the chariot. "Let us hope that Kupta and his men are drinking heavily tonight." He drew Temun aside. "How many stones can each of your men carry at one time."

"Two, three—four at the most," the headman returned.

"It is well. Let all but the wagon drivers take as many stones as they can carry for about eight hundred paces and follow us. You will remain here, should anyone come by. When the wagons are empty, you will order your men to drive them back to Nappa, and you yourself will come with your chariot to the spot where the stones will have been unloaded."

Temun nodded. The thought that he was about to see something unusual sent a chill through him.

Khiddon and Samson waited until Temun's men were laden with stones, then led the way across the hard-packed plain toward Kupta's town. Above it they could see a light reddish haze hovering in the air. The sounds of merriment came to their ears, and a moment later the walls of the town loomed ahead in the moonlight.

"This will do," whispered Samson. "The distance is right."

"As you say," replied Khiddon. He raised his hand to signal a halt. "Place the stones here, in a heap," he said to the men, "then go back to the wagons and fetch the rest, until not one is left." He bent down and scanned the pile. Nine or ten trips would do it.

As soon as the men turned back Samson picked up a stone and balanced it in the palm of his right hand. "These could have been a little larger," he remarked.

Khiddon laughed softly. "Never fear, young man. They will serve the purpose." Again he looked at the pile. "It would have been easier for the men if we would have brought the wagons here, but the risk would have been far too great. Any noise from this point would have brought the bandits out, and the whole plan would have been ruined."

It was after the men of Nappa had gone back for the sixth time that Samson, while taking a stroll around the plain to pass the time, saw a movement of something to his right, between himself and the walls of Kupta. He let himself down to the ground and remained there, motionless.

A moment later two figures came into view. They appeared to be staggering against each other, but clearly they were not drunk, for instead of sounds of merriment there came from their lips groans of pain.

The two did not see the boy crouching on the ground, but as they passed him, not more than three paces away, he stepped behind them and clamped his palms across their lips.

Khiddon came running to the spot. He looked the two men over. Their clothes were hanging on them in shreds, and blood was oozing from their bare arms.

"One outcry from you and it will be your last," Khiddon warned sternly. He motioned to Samson to relax his hold on the men. "You were thrown into the moat, is that right?" he demanded.

The men nodded painfully. "Three others are dead," one of them gasped weakly. "May a thousand curses fall on Kupta's head! May he fall into his own moat and die a thousand deaths there! May the wild beasts of the field feast on his carcass—"

"Enough of this!" ordered Khiddon. "Had you not broken the law of your city you would not be in this plight. Come along."

Temun's men were back with more stones. Khiddon called them aside. "Take these two back with you, and tell Temun to let them loose on the highway. They will not bother us." He looked at the retreating group. "Those two outcasts do not know how fortunate they are," he remarked to Samson.

Twice more the men of Nappa came with the stones. Then Temun arrived, cautiously leading his horse. The chariot rolled noiselessly along the ground.

The pounds of merriment in the town were dying down. Only two hours remained until dawn.

"How far from the moat would you say we are standing?" asked Khiddon.

Temun measured the distance with his eye. "About a hundred and fifty paces," he replied.

Khiddon picked up a stone. "Here is a—pebble," he said, placing it in Temun's hands. "Let us see how far you can throw it, with all your might."

The headman stared at the stone, then brought his hand up to shoulder level. With a strong heave he sent it flying. It landed with a thud some twenty paces away.

"Well done," cried Khiddon. "And now my nephew, being rather strong for one his age, will hurl a stone across the moat, over the walls and into the town."

Temun's jaw dropped. "I should have guessed that such would be your plan," he remarked ruefully. "Yet who would believe that there is anyone alive to perform such a feat?"

"Not anyone, not anyone, only my nephew," said Khiddon. He turned to Samson. "Are you ready, O son of my sister?"

"Ready, uncle," replied Samson, amused as always by the "uncle-nephew" that Khiddon had created.

"Very well," said the riddle-master. "Temun and I shall keep handing you the stones. Begin the attack!"

Samson gripped the stone and drew his arm back slowly. It came up again in a swift arc. The stone sailed high and landed a few paces from the moat. Without a word the boy reached for another missile. This time the thrust forward was a little more powerful. The stone flew up as from a giant sling, cleared the wall and came crashing down, with a splintering sound. Hardly had the echo of the first stone died away when the next one smashed into the town. One after another, aiming in an arc to his left and to his right, Samson sent the missiles hurtling.

A frightening uproar arose in Kupta's town. Shrieks and curses of pain, mingled with hoarse shouts, rose into the dust-filled night. Suddenly a column of fire began swirling upwards, sending sparks flying amidst a thick cloud of smoke.

Khiddon, working along with Temun to keep Samson supplied with stones, kept one eye on the walls. Why had the gates not been opened? Only a small pile of stones was all that that was left. If the rocky shower would stop, the entire plan could fail.

Then it happened. One after another the gates finally came open, as the frenzied bandits who had been pressing against them gave way enough to let them swing wide. But the terror that had seized the town was so fearsome that many did not wait for the planks to be rolled out and stretched across the moat. Clawing at each other like madmen they pushed through the gate and leaped into it. Others clambered up to the top of the walls, frantically searching the skies to see wherefrom the rain of stones was coming. Then a stone dropped in their midst, and the walls cleared as if by magic.

All this time Kupta, caught helpless in the panic that had seized his town, kept rushing from one gate to another, pleading with his men to keep their nerve up. In desperation he seized two of them and tried to drag them away from the gate. Before they knew what they were doing, the crazed bandits turned on their leader and clubbed him to death.

This act, and the sight of Kupta lying motionless on the ground, brought the bandits to their senses. The plank was placed on its wheels and rolled up to the gate, opposite the spot where Samson was standing, ready to hurl the last of the stones.

The glint of moonlight on the wheels caught Khiddon's

eye. "They are going to bridge the moat," he panted. "Do your best to hit that plank."

The boy took careful aim and let go. The stone, hurling low, missed the plank itself by a hair but struck the wheels. The impact gave the plank a thrust forward. It slid into the moat, just out of the desperate reach of the bandits, and flopped over to the farther bank. With wild shrieks the bandits slithered down into the moat after it.

"Look!" pointed Khiddon. Out of the moat, here and there, a few figures were painfully crawling up to the plain. "These are all that remain of Kupta's band of rogues. They will never return to their town, and all who had reascn to fear Kupta will need to have fear no more." He nodded toward the chariot. "Now let us depart for Timna. We shall remain there, while you, Temun, will go back to your village."

Temun shook his head. "No, no; both of you will come back with me. We shall hold a feast in your honor and reward you as you deserve."

But Khiddon refused. "Remember, Temun," he said. "Kupta and his bandits were thought of as heroes. Let it not be known that the men of Nappa brought about his downfall." He paused for a moment. "Tomorrow, Temun, you will take your blacksmiths to Kupta's town; should anyone question you, say that you had heard that an earthquake had visited it, and that you and your men had gone to see what could be done."

"But what shall we do there?" asked Temun anxiously.

"You will remove what has to be removed, quickly," replied Khiddon. "Then you will build your smithies there, so that your children in Nappa should not have lungs filled with soot and eyes smarting with smoke. And in the wall of your own smithy, Temun, you will set in one of the stones that caused the ruin of Kupta's town. You will also promise me now what I ask of you."

"Ask whatever you desire," replied Temun earnestly, "and I shall do it." Unseen in the darkness, his eyes had become moist.

"In your day, or in your children's day, if anyone should come—from anywhere, even outside Philistia— and point to this stone in your smithy and say: 'Is this the pebble of the nephew and his uncle?'—then, Temun, let him have anything he seeks—swords, spears, anything. Do you promise, Temun?"

"I promise," replied the headman of Nappa.

"Good. Let us then mount the chariot and be on our way to Timna."

The moon, tired of peering through the dust and smoke at the ruins of the town that was loud with merriment on that very same night, turned its attention to the chariot and its three occupants, bound northward on the deserted road. Then, ignoring the lonely jackal that kept howling at it far below, it went on along its starry course, high above Philistia.

The Ashkelon Fair

THE DRAY came rumbling through the gates of Ashkelon like a chariot, leaving in the air behind it a white trail of flour dust from the sacks packed between its boards.

The bystanders lounging at the gate scattered in all directions. "Take care, madman," one of them cried at the driver of the dray.

"Keep out of my way, fools," the driver flung back, adding a string of spicy curses. "When Perad drives, run for your lives."

The dray kept going up the main avenue until it came to one of the many side streets that led into the interior of the Philistine city. Perad swung the horse sharply into this narrow street, just as Khiddon and Samson stepped forth from the inn on the same corner. Only by leaping back at the very last instant did they avoid being run down.

"Careful, there," shouted Khiddon. "You will kill someone yet."

The driver, teeth bared in a wicked grin, hardly turned his head. "When Perad drives, run for your lives," he shouted back.

Samson's eyes flashed. "If I ever get hold of that one," he cried, "there will be one driver less in Philistia."

Khiddon gave the boy a playful nudge. "Let him be," he advised. "One of these days he will yell at a bird and land right in a ditch. Besides, we are not here in Ashkelon to deal with mad drivers but to see the famous Fair. Let us then be on our way."

They set off toward the Fair grounds, in the same direction that the dray had taken. Before long they saw it again, standing in front of a baker's shop.

Perad, followed by the baker, came out of the shop just as Khiddon and Samson drew near.

"Here are your twelve sacks," Perad said roughly to the baker. "Haul them off and pay me. I have other things to do."

The baker snorted. "You want *me* to take the sacks down?" he exclaimed. "That horse of yours has more brains than you have, imbecile!" He spat on the ground. "As long as the sacks are on your wagon the flour is not mine. You can take it back to the mill or choke with it, for all I care." With this, he turned about and went back into his shop.

"Dagon turn your flour into sand and your bread into stones," cursed Perad. He took hold of the top sack and dragged it down to the ground, grunting with every move. One by one he piled the sacks on top of each other, then went to call the baker.

Perad was hardly through the doorway when Samson was at the sack pile. One heave after another, as quick as the eye could follow, and the sacks were back on the dray.

The baker came out, with Perad on his heels. Both stopped short.

"Son of a donkey and father of a mule!" cried the baker. "Is this a game you want me to play with you? Are you a liar as well as a fool?"

Perad kept staring at the dray. He opened his mouth

but no sound came forth. Then, with a trembling finger, he pointed to the patch of white on the ground.

"I see, I see," cried the baker. "You have put some flour dust there. Wonderful! Now let me see; how many loaves of bread will I get from it?" His tone changed to a snarl. "Get those sacks down or I shall be buying from another mill."

Perad moved toward the dray. He was still so stunned that every sack now seemed to be tenfold its weight. By the time that the last one was down, poor Perad was gasping for breath.

"Aha! This is *much* better," exclaimed the baker. "Come inside and get your money."

When the two were out of sight Samson again edged toward the dray. This time he paid no attention to the sacks on the ground. Instead, he moved from one wheel to the next and gave each a gentle tug.

Perad came out from the shop, counting the coins in his palm. The money made him forget the strange behavior of the flour sacks. Again he counted it. There was enough for a big meal and a jug of wine at the tavern, a little to spend at the Fair, and perhaps a coin or two for some fodder for the horse. Perad climbed aboard the dray and made ready to move on.

The horse did not budge right away. He turned his head and gazed at Perad mournfully, as if to say: "You may not know it, O master mine, but while you were away from me—ah, well, what is the use!" For Perad had in the meantime reached for the whip, and the horse quickly decided to let matters take their course.

The dray moved off a pace or two. Then it happened.

Loosened at their hubs by Samson's "gentle" tug, the wheels slid off the axles and the dray, along with its shrieking driver, crashed to the ground.

A crowd gathered quickly, but instead of coming to the aid of the unfortunate driver the bystanders broke into loud jeers. Someone started to chant, "When Perad drives, run for your lives," and immediately the others joined in. Khiddon and Samson, by this time well away from the scene, could still hear the laughter behind them.

"Perad will be a changed man, I dare say," remarked Khiddon. "For this, Samson, every citizen of Ashkelon owes you a measure of thanks."

The Fair was in full swing when the two reached the market place. Gay banners fluttered in the fresh breeze above the shops and stalls. Red-faced hucksters stood over their wares, shouting their praises to the blue skies. In the food stalls dust and flies kept settling on the honey cakes and fruit clusters.

It was Khiddon's idea to find the area where strong men were to match themselves against each other for prize money, but no such area was in sight. He finally asked one of the shopkeepers.

"That will be this afternoon," the shopkeeper replied. "Our champion, Otzem, will meet the challenger from Gath, Anak."

"But what about the usual wrestling and weight-lifting?" inquired Khiddon. He had been hoping to have Samson win some prize money in the contests.

"Tomorrow will be time enough," replied the shopkeeper. "Today it will be between Otzem and Anak."

Khiddon was still pondering the situation when

Samson drew his attention to a group gathered about several men squatting on the ground. The riddle-master did not have to look twice.

"What you see there," he said slowly, "is known as the shell game. The one in the middle has two shells and a bead. He moves the bead on the ground from one hand to the other, then covers it with one of the shells. If you can guess under which shell the bead has come to rest you win one or more coins. If you do not guess right, your money is gone."

Samson tried to peer over the heads of the bystanders. "Is it so difficult to guess right?" he wondered.

Khiddon cleared his throat. "It depends on the dealer —that is, the one with the shells. The good ones—and I might say that all of them have to be quite good—move their hands and fingers about so swiftly that the eye cannot easily follow the movements."

Samson eyed his companion curiously. "Were you ever a dealer in this shell game?" he asked.

Khiddon's face twitched slightly, and a guarded twinkle came into his eyes. "The shell game," he replied, "is one that is played everywhere—along the caravan routes from the Nile to the Euphrates, in the courtyards of wayfarers' inns, and at fairs such as this one. And as one travels about, as I have done, one observes here and dabbles there, at times even becoming an expert—which I do not pretend to be."

"But is it a fair game?" probed Samson further.

"Indeed it is," Khiddon hastened to reply. "The dealer believes that the movements of his hands are too fast for the eye to follow, and he is ready to wager *his* money on it. Now there are many who believe that their eyes *can* follow the dealer's moves, and they are willing to wager *their* money against his. This is all that there is to the shell game."

Samson appeared to be puzzled, and Khiddon's smile deepened. "What else would you like to know about this game?" he asked.

"What I do not understand," replied the boy, "is who is right. If the hand *is* faster than the eye, how can anyone win the dealer's money? But if the eye is faster, how can the dealer win?"

Khiddon laughed heartily. "Such is the nature of a game of skill," he returned. "Not all of your dealers are skillful, nor is everyone's eye as swift as he might think. Of course, no one likes to lose money, and at times this little shell game can grow into a real battle." He paused, as though debating the matter with himself. "Come," he said finally. "Let us see how this game is going along."

The dealer, a slim, swarthy man with eyes as glittering as the bead that ran from one shell to the other, was squatting inside a circle of some twenty men. Directly in front of him was the player, whose looks and manner stamped him as a visitor from the countryside. In front of the player was a gleaming heap of silver coins.

"Ah, your eyes are sharp, my friend," the dealer was saying, and the soul of sadness was in his voice. "But how can I confess that my skill is gone? Come, one more wager. Fifty pieces against fifty pieces." With this he poured out a sack of coins on to the ground.

"Another victim," murmured Khiddon.

The villager evidently had more confidence in himself.

From inside his rough cloak he brought forth a handful of coins, which he added to those that he had already won. "Roll your bead," he cried. "My eye is like the eagle's."

As Samson watched intently, the dealer began shuffling the bead from one shell to the other with movements so swift that the boy from Zor'ah became thoroughly bewildered. He stole a glance at Khiddon; the riddle-master's lips were curved in an amused smile. In contrast, the look on the villager's face was one of utter panic. His eyes darted from side to side in a vain attempt to keep pace with the scurrying bead.

Finally the dealer stopped. "Where would you say, my dear friend, is the bead—under the shell in my right hand or under the shell in my left?"

The villager extended a shaky finger. "U-under your left," he stammered.

"Under my left you say?" repeated the dealer. He raised the shell slowly. The bead was not there.

A howl of laughter came from the bystanders. The villager looked about him in a daze, hardly aware that the dealer was gathering the bright coins into his sack. Then, as if in a trance, he rose and stumbled away.

"Who will now pit his eyes against my hands?" exclaimed the dealer. "Surely there is one here who is my master."

Samson nudged his companion. "Should I try?" he whispered.

Khiddon nodded. "Up to the point where you will have lost ten pieces," he replied. "Then you will tell the dealer that you have no more."

The long-haired boy moved forward so swiftly that

there was no mistaking his intention. The dealer spotted him before he had reached the circle.

"There, now," cried the dealer. "Young people always have sharp eyes, and here is one youth who might yet send me to the beggar's seat. Make room for him, good people, make room."

The bystanders needed no urging; it was always exciting to see the fools lose their money. They parted to let Samson through, and before they came together again Khiddon was squatting at the boy's side.

The dealer pushed two coins forward. "With two I start to work my art," he exclaimed in a singsong voice. "Match them if you care to play. Wager later if you dare."

Samson put his two coins on the ground and fixed his eyes on the dealer's hands. As they began to shuffle the bead to and fro he was surprised to see that he could follow their movements quite easily.

"Under the shell in your left hand," he cried when the dealer stopped.

"Hah! What did I tell you?" the dealer called out to those surrounding him. "The sharp eye of youth!" He raised the shell, and there was the bead.

Khiddon bent a little closer toward Samson. "Wager all you have," he said, hardly moving his lips.

Samson set down his remaining eight coins. "I am wagering twelve," he announced grandly.

"So?" cried the dealer. Samson's move caught him a little by surprise. The boy did not look as though he were laden with coins; still, one could not tell. The dealer therefore poured twelve coins from his sack next to Samson's pile.

Again the bead began rolling, this time a little faster.

"Left, left," shouted the bystanders, as it came to a stop.

Samson frowned. He was sure that the bead was under the shell in the dealer's right hand. He stole a glance at Khiddon's hands; the right one was twitching slightly.

"The right one," exclaimed Samson.

The dealer pretended to be overwhelmed. "The boy is remarkable," he muttered loudly. He raised the shell, and again, there was the bead.

Khiddon spoke up for the first time. "You may rest sure that my nephew is blessed with keen eyes." From inside his cloak he brought forth his money pouch. "I shall wager one hundred pieces of silver. Surely between us we should be able to follow the bead."

An excited murmur ran through the group. A hundred pieces of silver was a sum not to be disdained! All eyes were on the streams of coins that came pouring from the two sacks.

Once more the bead was sent from one hand to another, but this time Samson knew it was futile to even try keeping track of it, so swiftly did it fly between the dealer's fingers. When suddenly the movement stopped he did not have the faintest idea under which shell the bead was now resting.

"Where is it, my young friend?" the dealer asked softly.

Khiddon cleared his throat. "My nephew took his eye off the bead," he exclaimed sadly. "Therefore I shall have to venture a guess." He waited until the chatter of the crowd had died down. "The bead," he said, "is neither beneath the right shell nor the left shell. It is between the fourth and fifth finger of your left hand." Before the dealer could make a move, Khiddon's arm shot out and grasped him by the left wrist. Slowly the bead rolled out from between the dealer's fingers.

An ominous silence descended on the spot, and Samson at once sensed trouble. He half-rose to his feet, expecting some kind of an attack. Only Khiddon remained calm. In one swift motion he scooped the coins into his sack, then rose and moved quickly out of the circle, with Samson hard on his heels.

Out of the corner of his eye the boy saw two burly men at the dealer's side rise to their feet. Nor did Khiddon fail to see them. He hastened his pace and headed toward the rear of a cluster of tents off to one side of the market place. "We must get rid of them," he whispered tersely to Samson, "else they will stalk us until they get their friend's money back."

"What should we do?" asked Samson, casting a glance back over his shoulder. The two men were some thirty paces behind them.

"Let them catch up with us behind those tents," Khiddon answered. "It will then be your task to discourage them from following us. How this should be done I shall leave to you."

They managed to reach their goal well ahead of their pursuers. When the latter came upon them, the boy and his "uncle" appeared to be busy counting the coins.

"Give us the sack or we shall cut you into little pieces," one of the men threatened, advancing with one hand outstretched. In his other hand he wielded a long, wicked-looking dagger.

"P-put that away," stammered Samson. "Here is the money."

"Hah! That is much better," cried the dealer's hench-man, replacing the dagger in its sheath. "Let me have it, and you bumpkins can go back where you came from."

Samson held out the sack, but as the other's fingers were about to grasp it the boy let it drop to the ground. With the same motion he grasped the man by the arm and, with a mighty push against his chest, sent him crashing into his companion. As the two went down in a heap Samson was upon them. One heave catapulted them high in the air, and they came down with a thud that shook the earth.

"Enough," said Khiddon, with a glance at the writhing men on the ground. "They will not follow us. You have dealt with them as they would have dealt with both of us, and that is a lesson that they will never forget."

They picked their way past the ropes and tent pegs and found themselves at the edge of a large throng clustered about one of the bigger tents. Along the front of this tent, topped with a string of bright banners, ran a long wooden platform. Along this platform, wiggling to the tune of a merry band at one end, was a line of dancing girls. The spectators were clapping their hands in rhythm with the fifes and cymbals, and at the same time a clown in red and yellow kept throwing petals of flowers at the dancers.

Suddenly the music stopped, the dancers flounced down on the wooden boards, and a short fat man came bouncing out of the tent behind the platform.

"Nothing—nothing—nothing!" he shouted, waving his pudgy arms about his head. "Nothing that you have seen out here can compare with what awaits you *inside* the tent! One small piece of silver will get you there, my friends! One small piece of silver and you will be able to feast your eyes on the most beautiful girls in all Philistia."

At this the band burst forth once more into a tooting of fifes and crashing of cymbals. The dancing girls struggled to their feet and took up their wiggling. The barker tried to join them, just to add to the merrymaking. Unluckily he lost his footing and fell off the platform, much to everyone's delight, landing almost at Samson's feet.

The boy from Zor'ah found this very delightful, like a game. With an easy move he lifted the little fat man off the ground and tossed him back to the dancers. The barker landed none too hard and rolled to his feet like a playful bear cub. By following the curious glances of the bystanders he saw at once who it was that had performed the feat.

"Ah, you are strong for one so young," he addressed Samson. "For this you shall go into the tent as my guest, to see the prettiest maidens in all of Philistia".

Samson meant no insult, but he was in a mischievous mood. "I have seen prettier ones," he retorted, before Khiddon could stop him, "in the cow pasture."

Too late did the boy realize that he had made a bad mistake. The pleasant smiles on the faces of the people around him vanished and dark scowls appeared in their place.

The barker glared at Samson. "You have long hair, young one," he growled, "and even a longer tongue. One more remark like that about our Philistine beauties and you will find yourself with a tongue much shorter."

One of the dancers suddenly stepped forward. "His hair!" she screeched. "I want his hair for a wig."

"Good idea!" exclaimed the barker, sensing that here was something to excite the crowd. "We shall start with his hair, just to show him what might happen to his tongue."

Khiddon's heart sank. If Samson's hair were to be shorn off, all would be lost! He glanced quickly about him. Several men in the throng had drawn their daggers and were testing their edges.

Then Khiddon saw something else. Some thirty paces away, near one of the wells, a high pole was imbedded in the ground. Why it was there the riddle-master did not know, but it gave him an idea. He had but a moment in which to whisper a few words in Samson's ear.

"I want my wig," screamed the dancer, bouncing up and down. "I want my wig."

For a brief instant the bystanders looked up at the girl. This was enough for Samson. With a quick lunge he broke through the crowd. By the time anyone moved he was halfway to the pole.

"After him!" yelled the barker.

A score of men, daggers flashing in the sun, took up the chase. They did not advance very far. Samson had uprooted the pole from the earth and was swinging it in an arc in front of his body as though it were no heavier than a shepherd's staff.

"Come nearer," he invited, "and I shall break your heads and arms."

Khiddon breathed a little more easily, yet he well knew that the danger was still far from over. Samson could not stand there all day swinging the pole.

Just then a loud clanking came from the other side of the well. One of the guards, attracted by the commotion, came hurrying to the scene, the bugle at his side banging against his sword.

"What is going on?" he shouted. "Who dares disturb the peace?"

"It is this young villain," one of the men cried. Like his companions, he had quickly put away his dagger at the sight of the guard. "He is threatening to break our arms and bash in our heads with that pole."

The guard looked first at Samson, then at the pole in the ground, and his eyes grew wide. "You—you pulled up the pole?"

"These cowards were going to attack me," Samson retorted. He thrust the pole back into the hole with such force that the ground trembled.

The guard, mindful that many eyes were upon him, drew himself up to his full height. "You have damaged public property and threatened peaceful citizens," he exclaimed. "You shall be punished as you deserve. Come with me."

Only a warning look from Khiddon stopped Samson from yanking out the pole again. "I throw myself upon your mercy," the boy said to the guard.

"We do not stand for any nonsense in Ashkelon," was the stern reply. "Come."

A shout of approval came from the bystanders. The barker, not sure whether the turn of events was good for business, ordered the band to strike up again and urged the girls to wiggle a little harder.

Khiddon stood aside until the guard, with Samson meekly in tow, was well away from the scene. It took him but a moment to catch up with the two.

"I am the boy's uncle," he addressed the guard, in a voice laden with lament. "He meant no harm, I assure you."

The guard did not break his step. "Away!" he ordered. "Were I this wild one's uncle I would be ashamed to have anyone know it."

"But he is not to blame, I tell you," pleaded Khiddon. "Before you came, those men really meant to do him harm, with their daggers.

The guard gave Khiddon a dark look. "Keep talking thus," he warned, "and I shall take you along together with him."

Khiddon's face took on a most piteous look. "It matters not," he wailed. "I am responsible for my nephew. I swore to my dear sister, on her deathbed—"

"Quiet!" roared the guard. "Your sister on her deathbed does not interest me." Then he softened a little." "You will tell your story to our ruler."

They were now at the gates of a large courtyard, in the center of which stood a low, broad building. From the number of guards about, Khiddon judged this to be the home of Ashkelon's chief official.

The guard prodded Samson into a doorway. Khiddon followed closely on their heels. He was sure that Samson would be able to break away at any time, but the idea of meeting the ruler of Ashkelon appealed to him greatly.

A few paces farther inside the building a sentry barred their way.

"I am taking this one to Salmidar," the guard announced.

"Not now," returned the sentry. "The Council is in session."

"Today?" wondered the guard. "With the Fair going on?"

"Because of the Fair," replied the sentry. "Otzem is ill."

The guard gasped. "Otzem?" he repeated. "What will happen to the contest."

"That," said the sentry, "is exactly why Salmidar has called the Council into session. With Otzem ill we stand no chance of winning."

The guard shook his head. "Those Gathians will never let us forget it. They will say that we are afraid of their Anak. But surely we must have someone else—"

"Not one whom Anak will not be able to best in the match," replied the sentry, "otherwise the Council would not be in session so long. Besides, we have put up so much money for the Fair that, if word of this gets around, the cry of pain from our treasury will be heard from the Lebanon to the Nile." He gave Samson and Khiddon a searching glance. "Who are these two?" he asked curiously.

"A brash nephew and his stupid uncle," replied the guard. "Imagine it! I come to the market place and find this long-haired one swinging the hitching-post in his hand—"

"The hitching-post?" cried the sentry. "Are you drunk? It would take at least ten men to pull it out of the ground!"

The guard shook his head violently. "I tell you he was swinging the post back and forth."

Khiddon took a small step forward. "Indeed the esteemed guard is right," he said. "My nephew, who is exceedingly strong for his age, thanks to the good care that I have been taking of him, pulled the post out of the earth, which I assure you was hard-packed as rock, and he did it as easily as though it were a reed on the banks of a river."

The sentry gave Samson a quick look. "Wait here," he ordered. If what he had just heard was true, and with Otzem ill—

The door at the end of the corridor opened and a tall, broad-shouldered man came out. "What is going on here, sentry?" he demanded.

Instead of replying immediately the sentry hurried to the man's side and whispered into his ear. In the gloom of the corridor Khiddon could not see the expression on the listener's face, but there was no mistaking the change in his voice when he spoke again.

"You say you saw this with your own eyes?" he asked the guard.

"Yes, O noble Salmidar," replied the other eagerly. "As soon as I saw the post in his hand, I said to myself—"

"Enough for the present," Salmidar commanded. "I want the boy in the Council chamber."

Khiddon bowed low. "He is my nephew, sir, and a

little slow of speech."

"You may come too," Salmidar snapped. He waited for the two to enter, then followed them, closing the door behind him, much to the disappointment of both the sentry and the guard.

The five men in the chamber gaped at the newcomers, but Salmidar wasted no time. "We may have the answer to our problem, O men of the Council," he said. "I am told that this lad possesses extraordinary strength." He turned to Khiddon. "Is this true?"

"Indeed you are right, O noble ruler of Ashkelon," Khiddon replied vigorously. "Allow me to recount his feats of strength. Now when he was only five—"

"Some other time," Salmidar broke in curtly. "This afternoon, at the Fair, Gath will challenge Ashkelon's claim. Our champion, Otzem, has defeated Gath's strong men—all but Anak, who will be here to engage Otzem in a contest."

"And Otzem is ill," said Khiddon.

"Yes, Dagon has stricken Otzem with illness, one day too soon. We have other strong men in Ashkelon, but none to match Anak—unless this nephew of yours can bring a miracle to pass."

Khiddon waved his hand airily. "What is the nature of the contest?" he asked.

Salmidar replied. "Usually the challenger does not reveal his plans. The defending champion simply has to match whatever the challenger does and, if he is successful, he then performs some feat of strength which the challenger must equal, until one of the two does something which the other is unable to match."

Again Khiddon waved his hand. "It matters not," he said. "Whatever this Anak will perform, my nephew will outdo him."

Salmidar did not seem too pleased with Khiddon's show of confidence. "Speak not too rashly," he warned. "If your nephew conquers Anak he shall receive two hundred pieces of silver. If not, *you* will be flogged and both of you will be driven out of the city."

Khiddon did not flinch. "Not for the two hundred pieces of silver, O noble ruler of Ashkelon, but for the honor of your fair city my good nephew will lay Anak's glory in the dust." He stood there, looking as though *he* were the ruler of Philistia's great city.

ANAK, ACCOMPANIED by a horde of gay Gathians in a caravan of wagons and chariots, arrived in Ashkelon shortly after mid-afternoon. Confident that their hero would win the contest, the Gathians were even more overjoyed when they learned, as they came into the gates, that Otzem had fallen ill. Victory was now assured.

The Gathians did not head immediately for the sporting field, where the match between the strong men was to take place. They first paraded through the area of the Fair, waving their banners and shouting taunts at the crowds as they drove by.

Anak's chariot, as was to be expected, drew the most attention. Himself more than a head taller than any man either in Gath or in Ashkelon, Anak was the center of attraction because of what he was holding in his hands, as the chariot rattled through the city. It was a large ball of reddish-brown stone, so smoothly polished that the sun's rays bounced off its surface like blinding arrows. The colors of the stone blended well with the leopard skin that covered Anak from shoulder to knee.

All Ashkelon knew by this time that Otzem would not meet the challenger from Gath. The taunts of the Gathians angered them no end, but there was little they could do but glare at the newcomers in silence.

Then, just how no one knew, a rumor began to spread that Ashkelon had a new champion, someone whom Salmidar had discovered at the last moment. Many dismissed the rumor with a disgusted wave of their hands. Salmidar, they grumbled, simply wanted to be sure that there would be people on hand at the contest, at which Ashkelon would probably be represented by some well-digger or wood-chopper. Still, the rumor sent a thrill of excitement through the city, and at the appointed hour the sporting field was packed as if Otzem would have been in the best of health.

A circle some forty paces wide at its center had been drawn in the field. Around this circle all of Philistia, so it seemed, had gathered to witness the contest. The Gathians, as the visiting challengers, were seated at the very rim of the circle, where they kept up a steady chant of praise for their champion and of ridicule for his opponent—whoever he might be.

Anak did not show himself at once. First came his polished stone ball, resting on a leather cushion which four Gathians carried into the ring and placed at its exact center. Then came four others, carrying very long poles in perfectly upright fashion. A square straw mat was tied to the top of the poles, forming a canopy high above the ground.

Salmidar, seated on a wooden platform together with the dignitaries of Ashkelon and Gath, watched the scene with outward calm, but inside he was boiling with anger—at himself. How could he have been so stupid as to allow himself to be talked into letting a boy meet Anak's challenge! The contest should have been put off to another day, Fair or no Fair.

But it was too late. The city herald of Ashkelon was already advancing toward the center of the ring. He raised his arm for silence, and at once the huge throng became hushed.

"From our sister city of Gath," proclaimed the herald, "to challenge the champion of Ashkelon comes Anak the mighty one, descended of forefathers famed for their strength. Enter this circle of contest, O Anak, and let the air be filled with the praises of those who acclaim you."

A shout went up from the throng, with the Gathians leading the cheers. This was to be their day, and before the sun would set there would be a new champion. They rose to their feet and waved their arms high as Anak, flexing his muscles with every step, advanced to the center of the ring.

Again the herald called for silence. It was now the turn of Ashkelon's champion to be announced. But who would be he? Umrat—Sulkot—Begret? Strong men indeed, but none a match for Anak.

"Otzem, the strong one, having been stricken with illness," proclaimed the herald, "a guest who has accepted Ashkelon's hospitality has offered to meet the challenger from Gath. The name of this guest is Kafthor, and he comes from a faraway land. Enter this circle of contest, O Kafthor, and let the air be filled with the praises of those who acclaim you."

A gasp like the breath of the winter wind came from the crowd when Samson showed himself in the circle. His size, compared with Anak's huge frame, was cause enough for surprise, but this wasn't all, by any means. With Salmidar's consent, Khiddon had turned his best talents to give Samson an almost unbelievable appearance. Around the boy's forehead was a broad band of green cloth. From this band down to Samson's shoulders ran strings of colored shells. A crimson cape, held at the waist by a silver sash adorned with tinkling bells, reached down to a pair of yellow leather leggings.

But all this was not enough for the riddle-master. He was determined that his "nephew" should appear before the Philistines in all his glory. And yet he did not want him to become too well-known. He therefore touched up the boy's face with streaks of paint, so that even the townspeople of Zor'ah would not have recognized him.

But if Samson's appearance caused amazement among the onlookers, on Anak it had an entirely different effect. With a bellow of rage he strode to the platform where Salmidar was seated.

"What is this?" shouted the strong man of Gath. "Are you Ashkelonians making fun of me, of Anak? Am I a weakling of eighty that I should be matched against this—this painted monkey? I demand an answer."

Salmidar was prepared for Anak's outburst. Even as the strong one was making his protest, the herald came toward him. A moment and a few whispered words later saw Anak a changed man. The scowl on his face vanished and a broad grin came in its place. He raised his arms for silence.

"The Ashkelonians believe that this monstrous mouse is so strong that I shall receive five hundred pieces of silver if he loses," Anak announced.

Raucous cheers rose from the Gathians around the circle. Anak was known to be generous with his money; ah, yes, the taverns in Gath would be doing brisk business for a week.

The herald took charge once more. "And now," he boomed, "the mighty Anak will tell us the nature of his challenge."

Anak's thick fingers rested lovingly on the shiny stone ball. "Hear ye, O people of Ashkelon and you, my worthy opponent. The men with the poles will hold the mat, first at ten cubits above the ground then higher and higher. I shall fling this ball upwards, and I expect my worthy opponent to do the same—that is, if he can. If he cannot, let him go back and tend to his house chores."

Again the Gathians cheered wildly.

Anak looked about in satisfaction. "I want you people of Ashkelon to know that I am kind of heart," he cried. "Even if your—ha, champion, fails in the canopy test I shall let him try his luck in another feat of strength. He and I shall toss the ball back and forth. After each throw we shall take one step backwards. As I reach him with my throw, so will he have to reach me with his, else let him go and watch over the sheep in the pasture, for no strong man is he."

The Gathian picked up the ball of stone and stepped back one pace. This was the signal for the men with the poles to raise the canopy. Anak stepped forward, bent low and swung the ball back and forth between his legs with rapid motion. With a final heave he sent it spinning up to the canopy, reaching it with ease.

A burst of cheering greeted Anak's feat. The Gathian grinned broadly and, with an elaborate sweep of his hand, invited Samson to pick up the ball.

"If it is to play that you wish," said the boy to himself, "so shall it be." He bowed clumsily to Anak, almost falling down in the process, much to the amusement of the Gathians in the crowd.

A moment later Salmidar was cursing himself for being the biggest fool in the world. Otzem's substitute seemed to be having difficulty lifting the ball off the ground! Salmidar shot a baleful glance at Khiddon, but the riddle-master appeared to be not in the least worried. If anything, he seemed to be enjoying the scene.

Samson finally picked up the ball, rolling it up along his legs until it was at his waist. As he staggered toward the spot from which the ball was to be thrown, it seemed that the ball was carrying *him*. The look on Salmidar's face was not pleasant to behold.

"Kafthor" suddenly decided that something was wrong with the men holding the canopy. He sauntered from one to the other, eyeing each with grave suspicion. As he walked he began flipping the ball from one hand to the other, as though it were a small melon.

An excited hum rose from the crowd around the ring, and the grin on Anak's face turned into a scowl.

Samson went back to the throwing spot. Like Anak, he spread his feet wide and swung the ball between them. The weight of the stone seemed to draw him forward. He fell over, letting the ball roll away from him.

Again Salmidar looked at Khiddon, and the riddle-master obliged him with a sweet smile.

Samson retrieved the ball and tried again. This time he managed to swing it back and forth several times, but as he let go it hurtled not upward but back over his shoulder, and straight at Anak!

The Gathian jumped aside just in the nick of time, and the roar that he let out could be heard above the cries of the onlookers. Salmidar himself was so startled that he jumped up from his seat. Only Khiddon remained unmoved.

Samson, circling as far away from Anak as he could, now picked up the ball once more. This time there was no trace of the clown in his manner. He motioned to the men with the poles to hold the canopy as high as possible, some thirty cubits above the ground. Then, holding the stone in one hand, he heaved it upward with such force that it tore the mat right off the poles!

A mighty cheer rose from the Ashkelonians. This Kafthor a weakling? Hah, with one hand, too! And he caught the ball as it came down! Amazing!

Salmidar was now all smiles. He could have embraced Khiddon as a long-lost brother.

Amidst the Gathians there was dead silence. Their champion was being shown up by an undersized stranger whom no one had ever seen before.

Anak himself knew that he was beaten, but he was not

ready to give up. He watched silently as the men with the poles walked off the field, then picked up the ball from the cushion where Samson had replaced it and measured off five paces from the center of the ring.

Samson did the same, so that there were now ten paces between the two. He bent forward slightly, ready to receive Anak's first toss.

But the Gathian had something else in mind. Instead of tossing the ball he raised it high above his head and hurled it at his opponent, hoping to knock Samson down. Much to his chagrin, the boy merely held up one hand to stop the flight of the ball, which then dropped into the palm of the other.

It was now Samson's turn. His arm came up, and the ball went spinning in a high arc toward Anak. The Gathian hesitated, then stepped back and let the ball drop to the ground in front of him.

Hoots of derision broke from the crowd. This was more than Anak could stand. With a cry of rage he picked up the ball and hurled it at Samson with all his might, only to have the boy slap it down.

The crowd went wild. Cries of "go do your house chores" and "go tend to the sheep in the pasture" came at Anak from all sides. He turned toward Samson and went into a wrestler's crouch, but the sight of the stone ball bouncing up and down in the boy's hands caused him to change his mind.

Slowly the hapless challenger from Gath walked off the field, and the noise of the crowd died down. It was a sad sight to see shoulders as broad as Anak's droop so badly.

The herald's loud voice broke the spell. "It being that Kafthor has brought victory to Ashkelon," he proclaimed, "it is the decree of Salmidar that henceforth this be known as the Field of Kafthor, so that others may be inspired by his strength to do such feats as he has done this day."

These were pleasant words for Khiddon, as pleasant as the tinkle of coins in the sack that Salmidar had given him.

"There will come a day," the riddle-master said to Samson later, as they were resting in Ashkelon's finest inn, "when you will be back here in Ashkelon, and people will marvel at your strength. Still they will tell you: 'There was one here by the name of Kafthor. Ah, now *he* was a strong one . . . '"

Delila of Sorek River

"SOREK TAVERN," Khiddon read aloud the sign above the doorway of the rambling stone house. "Let us stop here." He slid wearily off his mule to the ground and motioned to Samson to dismount. They tethered their animals to the trough and went in.

"Mmm," muttered the riddle-master, as his gaze rested on the group in the spacious room. "I smell trouble."

Following Khiddon's look, Samson saw a half-dozen men clustered about the tall, burly figure of a Philistine warrior, young but rough-looking. By his helmet Khiddon identified him as a captain of "Dagon's Raiders," a special force set up by the Philistines to invade the territory of the Hebrew tribes and harass the inhabitants. Most of the Raiders came from the wealthier families in Philistia, for service with this force meant a lot of fun without too many risks.

The warrior in the center of the group, busy recounting the details of his latest raid, paid no attention to the newcomers. Khiddon and Samson, on their part, sat down at a table off to one side and waited for the tavern keeper to approach them.

"Be prepared to starve to death," muttered Khiddon to his companion. "The owner of this place doesn't dare leave while the brash one is telling his tales."

Samson half-rose from his seat. "I shall go and fetch him."

Khiddon's hand restrained the long-haired boy just in time. "Not so fast, young man," the riddle-master warned. "I know these Raiders. Interrupt their boasting, and they will cut you into small pieces."

Samson shrugged. "Anyway, we have a choice," he snorted. "We can die either of starvation or by the sword."

Despite himself Khiddon broke into laughter. At the sound, the Philistine stopped talking and swung around, frowning. "Who dares laugh at Yahir?" he demanded.

"Come, they're only travelers," one of the group called out. "On with your story."

Yahir gave the pair a baleful look, then turned back to the others. When he spoke again his voice was much louder — now that his audience had grown by two.

"We got those Hebrew jackals into the market place," he went on. "I said to them: 'I want you to be happy. Dance!' But they stood there, like chunks of stone. I then said: 'Wretches! Are you deaf or are you lame? Dance! Dance!' What do you think of that?"

The men surrounding Yahir laughed approvingly.

"When they still refused to move," continued Yahir, "I drew my sword from its scabbard and swished it at the feet of the Hebrew nearest to me. Hah, you should have seen how fast he moved!"

Khiddon stole a glance at his companion. Samson's face had turned pale, then red. His fingers clasped the edge of the table so tightly that the riddle-master was sure the board would break. "No rashness, Samson," he whispered. "You must use your head."

For an instant Samson did nothing, then a queer look crossed his face. Without a word, he folded his arms on the table, laid his head down upon them, and gave forth with a snore that could easily be heard above the voice of the Philistine.

Khiddon sighed. He well knew what was coming.

In two strides, Yahir was at Samson's side. He reached down, grabbed the boy by his hair, and yanked his head up. "No one sleeps while Yahir speaks," he snarled. "One more snore and I'll slice your head off."

Samson's eyes appeared to be glazed, but Khiddon, watching the boy closely, saw that his seemingly limp arm was doing something under the table. The riddle-master rose quickly and put his hand on Yahir's shoulder. "Come now, O noble captain of the valorous Raiders," he exclaimed. "Does it befit your station to be angered by a tired boy who has traveled so far that he can't keep his eyes open?"

The Philistine glared at the speaker, but his grip on Samson's hair relaxed. The boy's head dropped to the table again. As Yahir stalked back to his friends, Khiddon's eyes passed quickly over the lower part of his body, and a guarded smile came to his lips.

"Tell us more of your exploits," urged the riddle-master. "Better still, show us how you made those Hebrews dance."

The scowl disappeared from Yahir's face like magic. "I made them prance like frightened rabbits, I did," he exclaimed, reaching for his sword. "With one sweep—" He broke off suddenly and tugged at the weapon hanging at his side. It refused to come out of its scabbard. Again the Philistine tugged at it, this time a bit harder, to no avail. Now he yanked at it furiously, turning around and around like a dog in chase of its own tail.

The onlookers at first watched the scene with amazement. Then, as one man, they broke into wild laughter. The sight of Yahir, his face purple with rage, whirling crazily around and yanking at his sword like a madman, was too much for them. They howled with laughter until the tears came streaming down their faces.

"Dogs! Asses!" screamed Yahir. "I'll teach you how to laugh at me!" He managed to untie the belt around his waist and, with the stubborn sword still in its scabbard, he set about whacking his former friends until, screaming with pain, they ran out of the tavern.

Breathing hard, Yahir looked about. The tavern keeper was cowering in one corner; Khiddon and Samson were still at their table.

It suddenly occurred to the hard-breathing Philistine to examine his sword. He glared at it, then brought it nearer to his unbelieving eyes. There, slightly below the midpoint, the scabbard was crumpled as though it had been made of putty.

"Must have hit it against a stone or something," Yahir muttered to himself. Suddenly the scene of his laughing friends came to his mind. "I'll wring their necks," he shouted. With a sudden motion he threw the mangled scabbard into the empty fireplace and left the tavern.

The keeper, still quaking with fear, moved quickly toward the pair. "These Raiders," he muttered. "So bold, so rash, so —"

"—so forget about them," remarked Khiddon sharply. "Bring us food and drink—now!"

AN HOUR later, much refreshed, the two were on their way again, following the road between Ashkelon and Gaza along which ran a stream which the Philistines called Sorek. Its course was remarkably straight, almost like the flight of an arrow, and it continued without a break— except at one point, where a canal had been dug to join it. Thus some of the Sorek's waters entered the canal and flowed out to the estate of Takif.

Now not everyone could draw off water from the Sorek for his own use. Takif, not being just "everyone," could—and did, he being the wealthiest man in the region. The water coursed lazily along the canal and through a culvert beneath the wall surrounding the estate, flowing beneath the surface into a pool at the farthest end, where Takif and his friends were wont to enjoy themselves on hot days.

And Takif had many friends indeed. Hardly a day passed that did not witness a horde of guests sprawled out on the lawn, feasting around the cooking-pit or splashing about in the pool. Even the Governor of Gaza was known to leave matters of state lie simmering in the heat while he himself kept cool in Takif's pool.

There were many people, residents of Takif's native Gaza, who knew him when he was nothing more than a stonemason's apprentice. But even in those days he boasted more than once that, some day, he would be rich enough to do whatever his heart would desire.

Soon enough Takif was no longer an apprentice but

a skilled craftsman in the art of stonemasonry. At first he built dwellings for men of modest wealth. Then, as his fame spread, he was called to Ashkelon, Ashdod and the other Philistine cities, where he built fine dwellings for the army officers, the tax-collectors, and even the governors.

But the greatest of Takif's triumphs was the Temple of Dagon in Gaza. It was a truly magnificent edifice, designed as well as built by the former stonemason's apprentice. The main entrance, above which a giant stone carving of the god Dagon protruded from the wall, opened to the Great Sea, on the west. Along the walls, on either side, wide ramps zig-zagged up to the roof, which then sloped down gently on all four sides in long lines of tiers, over-looking the courtyard inside the Temple below. These tiers provided seating for three thousand and were always used by the plain townspeople, since the nobles and officials had their places on the main floor, under the roof, where they could escape the hot rays of the sun.

The roof itself was supported by two mighty cross-beams, which in turn rested on two stone pillars, set two paces apart. The polished granite pillars were so massive and so skillfully fashioned that Takif boasted that the Temple of Dagon would stand firm for a thousand years—if not forever.

Takif's reputation now knew no bounds. He now possessed much wealth—as he once boasted he would.

Takif had an only son, Hazuf, known in Gaza as "Takif's wild one." He and his equally adventurous friends liked nothing better than to ride their horses through the market place and knock over a few stands here and there. The merchants were somewhat angry—but not too angry, since Takif always paid for the damage that his "wild one" had caused.

Hazuf also liked to give parties, on his father's estate. For entertainment there was always the same main attraction—some new evidence of Hazuf's strength, for strong he was as an ox. And if his guests were inclined to be bored by the show they nevertheless managed to keep their boredom well-hidden, lest they never again be invited to enjoy the food, the pool, and the reputation of being "somebody."

Now Khiddon and Samson had never heard of either Takif or his offspring, nor did they have any plans to visit the estate. What led them to its gates was the canal. Khiddon was curious to know where it went and why. As for Samson, it was enough for him that his companion was curious, since this always led to an adventure of some kind.

The pebbly road leading to the estate rose slightly as it neared the gate, leaving the canal just below its level, where it disappeared through the culvert beneath the wall.

"He who dwells within," remarked Khiddon, letting his eyes rove from one end of the wall to the other, "must be a man of means. Certainly he does not need the water for drinking, when a well would be much better. Let us find out."

Several paces on the other side of the iron-grill a servant in a loose-fitting cloak was working among the shrubs.

"This one does not look like the answering kind," muttered Khiddon, noting the sour look on the servant's

grizzly face. "Still, we shall not be punished for trying."
He leaned against the gate, rattling it slightly, and put
on his best smile. "Ah, my dear man, can you—"

The startled servant looked up. "Away with you," he
called out. "We need no beggars here!"

Khiddon drew back a step and from his cloak brought
forth his money pouch. "If we be beggars, my dear man,"
he exclaimed, jingling the pouch vigorously, "at least we
are not poor ones, eh? Now, a silver coin will be yours if
we can have a chat with you."

The servant clomped out of the shrubbery and came
toward the gate. "What do you want?" he demanded.

"We are entertainers," Khiddon returned, "and the
coin will be yours if you tell your master we are here."

The servant's face turned even more sour. "My master," he retorted, "needs no wandering fools." He eyed
the sack of coins and moistened his lips. "What kind
of entertainment do you do?"

"Ah, that is better!" exclaimed Khiddon. "As soon
as I laid eyes on you I knew that you are indeed a man
with a mind of his own. Let me therefore tell you that
I am a riddle-master, while my friend here performs
feats of strength not seen in all of Philistia."

The servant's look shifted to Samson. "A strong
lad, eh?" he cried. "So is the son of my master." He
looked about carefully and came closer to the gate. "Is
this one really strong?" he whispered.

"You doubt my word?" Khiddon cried—but not too
loudly. The change in the servant's manner was most
unusual. "Tell us more about the son of your master."

Again the servant glanced around. "Hazuf is strong

indeed. No one of his own age, and few of his elders, can match his muscles. Therefore Hazuf is much taken with himself and boasts of his strength night and day. It is time that he be taught a lesson."

Khiddon raised his hand. "Say nothing more, my good man," he exclaimed. "If somehow a match can be arranged between your Hazuf and my friend here, with a sizable wager to go along with it, you might find yourself with a tidy little sum."

The servant shook his head. "I look for no trouble," he said. "Right now Hazuf is entertaining some of his friends on the lawn behind the house. I can only tell him that there is a challenger at the gate who wishes to pit his strength against him." He cocked his head to one side. "Just how strong *is* this lad?"

Khiddon looked about for something to test Samson's strength. His eye paused on the gate. It was made of iron, so heavy that the smiths who had fashioned it had merely dropped the hinges into the sockets, without bothering to fasten them. "If you will step back, my dear man," he advised the servant, "my friend will demonstrate his powers, and at the same time you will be spared the work of opening the gate."

The servant obeyed, and the puzzled look on his face gave way to a gasp of astonishment as Samson, with a firm grip on the grill-work, eased the hinges up and out of their sockets, and then, swinging the gate sideways to let himself and Khiddon through, replaced it with equal ease.

"Now, my dear man," the riddle-master addressed the servant, "how do you think the match will come out?"

The man's jaw still hung limp. "I—I shall go fetch the son of my master," he finally managed to say. He trotted away, looking back over his shoulder to make sure he wasn't dreaming.

Khiddon shook his head. "Perhaps I should have chosen something more simple," he sighed. "You may have to lift the gate again to convince young Hazuf."

Takif's "wild one" was now coming toward them, followed by the servant. He was indeed very well-built. The muscles of his body rippled smoothly; for this reason he went about bare to the waist, Khiddon was sure. But the face above the powerful neck, with its beaked nose and small eyes, was not pleasant. Samson took an instant dislike to him.

"What am I told?" rasped Hazuf. "One of you lifted the gate off its sockets?"

"The gate?" Khiddon's blank look was a masterpiece of pretense. This Hazuf would be too clever to accept the challenge of anyone capable of the feat. "Ah, now I know! Your servant must have told you that my young friend *could* lift up the gate—with a little help, of course, heh, heh! But if you are ready to accept a challenge—"

"Enough!" bellowed Hazuf. He gave the luckless servant a shove that sent him sprawling to the ground. "Now you two beggars get out of here and keep away, or I shall crack your heads together like a pair of hen's eggs."

Before either Khiddon or Samson could reply a young girl came running toward the gate. Samson's eyes opened wide. Her hair was like golden flax, and it was even prettier with the garland of blue flowers around it. Her dark eyes were unusually round, and when her lips opened to speak, Samson beheld the most perfect white teeth that he had ever seen.

"What is going on, Hazuf?" she asked breathlessly. "Why did you leave us?"

"A pair of wanderers, Delila," replied Hazuf, "on their way out."

Khiddon bowed to the girl. "Forgive us, young mistress, if we annoy you," he said, in his sweetest tone. "Indeed we are on our way out, for we must be in Gaza, where my young friend here will challenge the strongest men in the city to a match."

Delila looked at Hazuf. "What does he mean?"

Hazuf hesitated. This wanderer was a clever one! And about the gate—could the servant have been right? Impossible! And yet—

"Come back tomorrow," he said hurriedly, knowing well that Khiddon's next words would be a challenge to himself.

"If you are not afraid to match strength, it will be now or not at all!"

This was Samson who spoke, and Khiddon looked at him in amazement. This was the first time that the boy from Zor'ah had spoken in such blunt fashion. Then the riddle-master caught the direction of Samson's gaze, and immediately he understood. For the boy, though addressing himself to Hazuf, never took his eyes off Delila.

The girl clapped her hands in delight. "Accept his challenge, Hazuf," she cried. "He has long hair, but surely you are the stronger one."

Hazuf looked Samson over from head to foot. *He* lifted the gate? Impossible! "Very well," he agreed. "We shall have some sport. You," he turned to the servant, "will bring my things to the lawn."

The things turned out to be an assortment of iron stakes, ropes and weights. These the servant dragged out to the lawn behind the mansion, where some ten young gentlemen and maidens were gathered.

"We have some fun here," announced Hazuf, his small eyes darting back and forth over the group. "This fellow has challenged me to a match of strength."

Loud laughter greeted the remark. "He must be either a stranger," one of the boys exclaimed, "or a fool—or both."

Khiddon seated himself at the edge of the grass and waited. This was going to be for Samson to carry on, in any way he saw fit.

Hazuf picked up one of the iron stakes. "For a start," he said, "I shall bend this a bit, and my challenger will attempt to straighten it out—if he can." He flexed his muscles, set his feet wide apart and, gripping the stake, bent it almost double, to the delighted handclapping of his friends. "Your turn, O mighty one," he turned to Samson. Instead of handing the stake to the long-haired boy, however, Hazuf flung it, with a scornful toss, into the grass beyond the group.

Samson made no reply. He went to the spot where the stake had landed, but for some reason he appeared to have a great deal of trouble locating it. The spectators broke into laughter as he went down to his knees in search of the stake. Delila laughed the loudest of all.

At last Samson found what he was looking for. But was it the stake that Hazuf had bent? For the one that Samson was now holding was perfectly straight! "I do not know where yours went," he said to Hazuf in a most perplexed tone, "but I found this one."

"Find the other!" Hazuf roared at the servant. Khiddon, inwardly laughing so hard that his body shook, watched the others join in the fruitless search. The riddle-master had the feeling that this was not going to be one of Hazuf's better days.

The "wild one" finally called off the search. "It matters not," he remarked with a disdainful wave of his hand. "We shall reverse the matter. My noble challenger will bend the stake, if he can, and I shall show him how easily I shall straighten it out."

"My heart weeps for you," Khiddon said to himself.

Samson accepted the stake gingerly and looked it over, frowning so deeply that Hazuf's friends again brayed with laughter. They howled with glee as Samson appeared to be wrestling with the bit of iron. He first held it close to his chest, then twisted his body completely around, gasping and groaning like a bear caught in a trap. Delila laughed until the tears came streaming down her cheeks.

At last Samson seemed to be completely exhausted. He staggered toward Hazuf and held out the stake, for all to see.

There was a gasp, followed by dead silence. Impossible! The iron stake was tied in a double knot!

Hazuf moistened his lips. He could not believe his own eyes—and he felt the eyes of his friends upon him. "You are no strong one," he hissed at Samson. "You are a worker of witchcraft—you and your friend. Now both of you—on your feet and be gone, else I shall have you driven off."

"Now if we are magicians. . ." began Khiddon, but Delila did not let him go on. She ran up to Hazuf and gave him a blazing look of scorn. "You are not being fair," she cried. "If you cannot perform your part of the feat, let it go!"

"He is not stronger," snarled Hazuf. "He is a magician from some foreign land. You see he is not one of us. We want no stranger here, do we?"

An angry growl came from the young men in the group, and Khiddon decided that it was time for him to take a hand in the matter. "Indeed you are right," he said to Hazuf. "We are from another land, which means that you are still the strongest young man in Philistia. Now, if you truly wish to entertain your friends I can pose riddles before you that—"

"We have no use for your amusements," Hazuf retorted haughtily. "Today my friends will witness my dive from the top limb into the pool, through a hoop of fire." He paused for a cheer from his friends. "Now off with you."

Khiddon motioned to Samson to obey. As the boy turned to go he found Delila by his side. "O strong lad from a distant land," she whispered softly, "when you come by here again, ask for me, at the house beyond the Sorek, where the canal begins. Will you?"

All Samson could do was nod, for his mouth had suddenly gone so dry that he could not utter a word. Khiddon took hold of his arm and gently guided him through the gate. "Young man," the riddle-master said sternly, "it appears that the charms of this Philistine girl have captivated you somewhat, eh?" He chuckled at the red flush that mounted to Samson's cheeks. "Ah well, you will probably never set eyes on her again."

The two were now about a hundred paces from the gate, along the path leading back to the highway. Suddenly Samson stopped. "That dive through the ring of fire," he replied to Khiddon's questioning look. "I should like to see it."

Khiddon glanced at the canal. The flow of water was at a standstill. "I think," he mused aloud, "that the water feeds into the pool which our pleasant young friend mentioned. Now, if the water is to remain fresh it must be changed from time to time. This can be done only by emptying the pool and allowing fresh water to flow in. For the pool to be drained it must have an outlet somewhere outside the estate. It is therefore my guess, my dear Samson, that if we make our way around the wall we shall find a stone plugged into it, a low patch of moist ground and probably a thousand flies."

The riddle-master was right in every detail, including the flies. Into the wall, directly at the other end of the estate, a large wheel-shaped stone had been set. Imbedded into this stone were four iron rings, by the means of which the stone could be pulled out, a sizable task for two strong men.

"We can look over the wall by standing on the rings," Khiddon remarked.

The two drew themselves up and cautiously peered over the top. There, below them, was the marble-lined pool itself, large enough for a score of bathers and more. About ten paces beyond its rim was a tall tree, its limbs spreading in all directions. Those closest to the pool had been stripped of their branches. It was from the highest of these that Hazuf was evidently planning to make his dive.

Samson lowered himself to the ground and stepped back a few paces, letting his gaze rest on the stone plug.

"Now, now, my young friend," said Khiddon quietly. "Can it be that you intend to pull out the stone and drain the pool just as Hazuf is about to dive? May I inform you that such action might well cause Hazuf to crack his skull or break his legs. This would cause Delila to grieve, and this is not desirable, is it?"

Again Samson's cheeks turned red, but this time he had a ready answer. "I shall not empty the pool," he returned. "If anything, I shall make it softer for the noble Hazuf to land, whether it shall be with his head first or his feet."

Khiddon watched curiously as Samson proceeded to claw into the moist earth at his feet, ripping up chunk after chunk. As soon as he had a sizable mound Samson cradled the chunks in his arm, climbed up with them to the top of the wall and let them drop noiselessly into the pool. Then he unplugged the stone and let some water out.

Khiddon shook his head in mock despair. "Ah, Samson!" he exclaimed. "When we left Zor'ah you were a simple, innocent boy. We have been in Philistia only a few weeks, and already you are a scheming young devil."

"You," retorted Samson, grinning, "are my teacher."

The riddle-master pretended to wince. "Ah, it is too

late now," he remarked. "The deed is done. There is nothing left to do but watch in silence."

They did not have to wait long. The sound of gay laughter on the other side of the wall came their way. Then, as Hazuf began his climb, everyone grew quiet.

Samson listened closely to Hazuf's grunts. The "wild one" was no coward. He was going to dive not only from quite a height but through a fiery hoop as well. Already the sharp smell of burning pitch came floating over the wall.

"The noses of Hazuf's guests are paying the price for the performance," whispered Khiddon. He drew Samson close to the wall so that Hazuf, now climbing higher, would not see them.

Hazuf reached the highest limb. He straightened up and stood there poised for a moment. With a final push against the swaying limb, he leaped.

The dive was perfect. Hazuf hit the burning hoop exactly in the center, amidst the wild handclapping of his friends. The splashing water put the fire out, but Hazuf did not come up immediately. When he did, he was coated from head to foot in a thick layer of mud.

The others stood there as though turned to stone. Then Delila began to laugh, a bubbly laugh that pealed through the air like a thousand kittenish bells. One by one the others joined in, some falling to the ground in helpless merriment.

Hazuf washed his face clear of the mud and clambered out of the pool. For a moment he stood there, fists clenched and face distorted with rage. "Out! All of you!" he finally cried. "Be gone before I break your every bone, by Dagon! Out!"

Khiddon and Samson skirted the wall for a while until they reached the canal.

"Such is the course that life takes," sighed the riddle-master. "Now you have everything, then you have nothing. One moment Hazuf commands the admiration of his friends, then, thanks to your bed of mud, he is the object of their ridicule. And that Delila! She is one to beware of, for her heart flits from one thing to another."

Samson didn't quite understand what Khiddon meant, but he kept silent. They were now by the bridge across the Sorek River, just where the canal joined the stream. A hundred paces beyond that point was a fine-looking house. In the doorway Samson thought he saw someone with flaxen hair encircled with blue flowers. He looked again, but this time there was no one in the doorway. With a quiet sigh Samson fell into step with Khiddon, to the spot where their patient mules were waiting.

Khiddon, the Godly One

THROUGHOUT PHILISTIA, the name of Khiura was rarely mentioned without a titter, a hearty laugh or a knowing smile. But in Ekron, one of the five capital cities of the Philistines, one had to be careful.

For Khiura was the daughter of Patish, governor of Ekron and one of the most powerful men in the land. She was born when Patish already held that important post, and she therefore had whatever her heart desired.

Patish's time was taken up with looking after his city. Since his wife's death years earlier, Khiura's upbringing had been left to the maids in the palace. Khiura was indeed fortunate if she saw her father a few minutes each day.

But the time came for Khiura to have a husband, and suddenly Patish discovered that he had quite a difficult task on his hands. True, his daughter had wealth, station and other things to offer, but beauty was, alas, not among them. Yes, the sad truth was that Khiura was as far from being a beauty as the sunrise was from the sunset. Her fondness for sweetmeats had rounded her figure to the shape of a barrel. Her face was covered with dark fuzz, which she vainly tried to hide beneath layers of powder. Khiura therefore rarely ventured forth from the palace in daytime except in her palanquin.

Many years passed by. As still no one came forward to ask for Khiura's hand, her father's spirit grew more and more troubled. To his fellow-chieftains—those with unmarried sons—he kept hinting that whoever would wed Khiura would some day certainly be governor of Ekron—but to no avail. Not a single young nobleman was willing to invite the jeers of his comrades, even if he were to be offered ten times that which Patish was offering!

The ruler of Ekron tried other measures, each more desperate than the others. He announced that he would give his daughter to the best athlete in Philistia; promptly all the good athletes became disinterested in sports. Khiura was then offered as the prize for the bravest warrior, at which the talk in the market place had it that the Philistine armies would be made up entirely of cowards.

Strangely enough, Khiura herself did not give up hope at all. Not for a moment did she doubt that one day a noble prince would come knocking on the palace gates to ask her father for her hand. After all, she had Yidonit's word for it.

Yidonit was a fortune-teller. She and her two servants, a man and his wife, lived in a fine house on the other side of the market place. Around the house ran a high stone wall, and inside the house itself was a small square court-yard, screened by a wooden vine-covered lattice. It was in this courtyard that Yidonit peered into the future to tell the fortunes, good or bad, of those who came to her.

In the center of the courtyard was a low round table. On its polished black surface were small heaps of sand, ashes, pebbles, feathers and dried seaweed. Hanging from a brass rod above the table were two bird cages, one white and the other black. In the white cage was a black raven.

In the black cage was a white dove.

A visitor seeking to have his fortune told would be seated three paces away from the table. Yidonit always began by kneeling on a green-and-red cushion at the table and calling on Dagon, Baal-Zebub and the other Philistine gods to answer her chants. This done, the visitor would state the purpose of his visit. If he wanted to know whether something good would happen to him, Yidonit would release the dove. If he expected some evil to befall him, Yidonit would release the raven. In either case, the bird would circle about the courtyard, then, swooping down over the table, flap its wings, causing the small heaps of sand to scatter. This done, the bird would return to its cage, while Yidonit, reading the signs, would tell the visitor what the future held in store for him. She never made the mistake of speaking plainly, so that the visitor would go away more confused than ever but at the same time thoroughly convinced that Yidonit knew more about the future than any fortune-teller in Philistia.

Yidonit was now wealthy and had every comfort she wanted, but it had not always been that way. Her star did not rise until Patish became the ruler of Ekron, and it happened in this manner:

Shortly after the old governor of Ekron died, the rulers of the other Philistine cities gathered to choose a new chief for the city. They met in the palace of the governor of Ashdod, overlooking the Great Sea, as was their custom.

Yidonit, a native of the seaport, was hardly more than a girl at that time, and more of a beggar than a fortune-teller. She wandered from one tavern to the next, from the market place to the caravan stations, offering to tell fortunes in return for a copper coin or a morsel of food.

The night that the Philistine chieftains met it was bitter cold and rainy. Yidonit, shivering in her tattered clothes, was returning to her hovel at the edge of the town when, passing by the palace, she saw that the gate was ajar. From somewhere inside the grounds came the clatter of dishes and Yidonit was very hungry. She slipped through the gate, passed unnoticed by the palace guards huddled in the doorway, and descended a short ramp that led to the kitchen quarters.

She heard voices coming toward her. Just a step farther was a narrow flight of stone steps leading to the upper floor of the palace. Yidonit quickly went up the stairs and along a dark corridor until she came to a large door, from beyond which came loud though muffled voices. By putting her ear against the door Yidonit could make out the words quite clearly. And thus it came about that, except for the chieftains in the room, Yidonit was the first to know that Patish was to be the new governor of Ekron.

The name of the new ruler meant nothing to the ravenous, hungry fortune-teller, but she at once grasped the opportunity that fate had thrown into her lap. Quickly she made her way out of the palace. The rain was still coming down in sheets, and the streets were deserted. Yidonit did not pause until she arrived, panting and breathless, at the home of her brother, a poor wood-cutter. He was resting from his day's toil when she rushed in, but there was to be no rest for him *that* night. Yidonit bade him get ready his mule and cart. They were going to Ekron.

When the merchants of Ekron arrived at the market place in the morning to open their stalls they beheld a strange sight. Around and around the public well in the center of the market place, a bedraggled, wild-haired woman kept circling and chanting, circling and chanting. When the number of the curious grew sufficiently to her liking, Yidonit called out that Dagon had revealed to her a secret: a man named Patish would be the next governor of Ekron.

The crowd jeered at the fortune-teller. Patish was known as a warrior; he had never been so much as the head of a village. But Yidonit paid no attention to the jeers. She kept throwing dust and pebbles into the air; they showed that Patish was the man. So said Dagon!

Some two hours later a herald came from Ashdod with the news of Patish's selection. Immediately the market place was in an uproar. Yidonit found herself surrounded by a huge throng, clamoring for her to remain in Ekron. Ah, here was indeed a true seer of the future! Yidonit was a clever one; if the new governor would so order it, she said, she would make her home in his city.

Patish not only ordered it. He also had a fine house built for her, and from that day on Yidonit had not a care in the world. Year after year went by, and all that changed was the growing hoard of gold and silver that Yidonit kept hidden somewhere in the house. No thief ever dared break in, for Yidonit had forewarned Ekron that whosoever would enter her home uninvited would be stricken by Dagon with every malady known to man.

Of all the visitors who came to see Yidonit—after

proper arrangements had been made, of course—none was more welcome than Khiura. The young lady was sure that the prince of her dreams would appear some day, but she did not wish to be caught unawares. Every morning, therefore, after a breakfast large enough to satisfy the hunger of a whole family for a whole day, Khiura climbed into her palanquin and ordered her slaves to bear her to Yidonit's home, where the white dove of the crafty fortune-teller always managed to stir up encouraging omens on the shining black table in the courtyard.

On this particular morning Khiura awoke with a song pounding in her heart. Again the vision of her prince had come to her during the night. He was tall and handsome, with sparkling black eyes and a merry tongue and a voice that rang like a bell wafted across the clear waters.

For the better part of an hour, while her maids were attiring her with her beaded cloak and spangled sash, Khiura kept debating with herself. Should she go to see Yidonit or not? What if the sand and the ashes and the feathers and the seaweed would show not a tall stranger with black eyes but some squat Philistine with eyes of blue or brown?

Khiura finally made up her mind. She would go to Yidonit as was her daily custom, else the fortune-teller would be cross, but she would hold back telling her about her vision.

So thrilled was the heavy maiden with her own bright idea that she tripped while getting into the palanquin and almost flattened it, along with the slaves under its poles. This so unnerved her that she leaned back against the cushions and closed her eyes, even though it was her habit to peer through the slit in the curtains for a glimpse of what was going on in Ekron along her route.

Arriving in front of Yidonit's door the slaves lowered the palanquin to the ground, waited until the fortune-teller's servant had helped Khiura descend, then went off to rest in the shade of a nearby tree. Like Patish, they prayed that some one—*anyone*—would come and take Khiura off their hands!

It was precisely at this very moment that Khiddon and his young companion were passing through Ekron's west gate.

At first they were going to by-pass the city. The time which Khiddon and Manoakh had set for Samson's stay in Philistia was almost up. The boy was eager to see his parents again, and Khiddon also felt a yearning to see the meadows of his native Gilead. However, early that morning, at the wayside inn where they had spent the night, the two travelers had come upon a most interesting bit of news.

Patish, they learned, wanted to plant a garden on a tract of land just to the north of his palace. This tract was overgrown with a forest of trees. In order that this be done quickly he sent word to all the strong men in Ekron to meet on a certain day in the market place: whoever would undertake to complete this task in not more than two weeks for the smallest sum would be given the job. Khiddon and Samson decided to head for Ekron. The riddle-master was sure that none could outbid them as far as the price went. As for the two weeks, Khiddon had no doubt that in less time than that Samson could uproot half the cedars in Lebanon.

Samson also favored the idea. After all the strange adventures that had befallen him in Philistia he was glad to do something that called for simple strength. Besides, he wanted to earn more money for his parents and the poor people of Zor'ah.

The two companions did not have to ask about the route to Ekron. Even before dawn the main highway to the city was alive with traffic feeding in from all the country roads leading into it. Mules laden with farm produce patiently plodded alongside flocks of sheep and slow-gaited camels, veering off the road every now and then to make room for creaking wagons and rattling carts.

By the time that Khiddon and Samson passed through the gates, the sun was already high in the sky, on its way to the noon hour and the meeting of the strong men in the market place. And indeed, as Khiddon's gaze swept across the busy area, there was a pompous-looking official standing on a slight rise, a scroll in his hand and a group of burly men around him.

"Over there," nodded Khiddon, "is where we shall earn a small fortune."

They made their way past the stalls and stationed themselves as close to the official as they dared, just as that gentleman was clearing his throat for the third time.

"Now, men of Ekron," he began, "give me your attention as I read this proclamation by His Excellency, Governor Patish."

A low growl came from the bystanders. "We know what's in it," one of them cried. "On with the bidding."

"It is my solemn duty," protested the official, but his words were drowned out by the impatient cries of the throng. He sighed, shaking his head. This was highly irregular, to say the least, but seeing that the protests were from the strongest men in Ekron . . .

"Very well," he agreed. "I shall proceed to accept your bids on the work that the noble Patish wishes to be done, in his desire to beautify our city. As you well know, the contract will go to him who, within not more than two weeks, will finish the work and do it at the smallest cost to our Governor. Now I believe that all of you are familiar with the size of the patch of ground where the work is to be done and with the number of trees to be removed. I do not want the successful bidder to complain later that he did not know there was so much work to be done."

A ripple of laughter came from all sides, and the brawny workmen winked at each other. This official knew his people very well.

"I ask that you men take my words seriously," he continued, rustling through the scroll in his hand. "Ah, yes. Let us not overlook the point that the uprooted trees are to be laid out in orderly fashion across the narrow ravine to the east of the wooded tract, so as to form a bridge. Also, the holes made by the uprooting of the trees are to be filled up and the ground leveled."

A growl of dismay arose here and there, and one or two of the would-be bidders drew back. This the official pretended not to notice. He was anxious to get through with his duties. The day was becoming hotter with every passing minute, and he had pleasant visions of a pitcher of date juice in the coolness of his favorite tavern. He rolled up the scroll. "Each of you," he went on, "is to write his name and the amount of the bid on a piece of parchment, roll it up and hand it to me. I shall read the names and bids as I unroll each piece. You may choose one from your midst to see whether I can still read correctly."

"Ah, we trust you," came from the others, but Samson saw that they lost no time choosing one of their number to stand right by the official's side.

"My bid will be the lowest," one of the men said in a hoarse whisper that could be heard halfway across the market place. "With my three strong sons and even stronger mules I can afford to outbid anyone."

"Hah! Are you not overlooking me and my four brothers?" snorted another would-be bidder. "All Ekron knows that when it comes to real strength, none can match ours."

Khiddon had in the meantime written something on his piece of parchment and handed it to the official. With the other bids it went into a reddish clay jar.

"Any more bids?" asked the official. Seeing and hearing none, he thrust his hand into the jar and brought forth the first bid: "Shurbosh and his sons agree to do the work for sixty-six pieces of pure silver."

Shurbosh was so certain that his bid would be the lowest that he began loosening his muscles, as though preparing to uproot the trees right then and there. His three sons, each of whom appeared to have more brawn than brains, took to aping their father's movements.

And indeed, as the parchment pieces were unrolled,

it seemed that Shurbosh's bid *was* the lowest. The next three were higher—not by much but higher nevertheless.

"The final bid," said the official, looking down at the parchment in his palm, "is from Khiddon and Company. The amount is—" He almost dropped the piece, then showed it to the man next to him. "Where are you, Khiddon?" he shouted.

The riddle-master stepped forward. "At your service, Excellency."

The official, vastly pleased at being thus addressed, still thought it best to scowl. "What kind of Company is yours?"

Khiddon bowed. "I employ neither sons nor brothers, only men with strong backs who are not afraid of work."

"And you have seen the clump of trees?"

"I have."

"And you are still willing to do the work for *forty-four* pieces of pure silver?" demanded the official.

A howl of disbelief came from the other bidders. Shurbosh let out such a bellow that people in the market place, thinking that a bull had been let loose, began to scatter in all directions. "Pay no attention to this crazy bid," he yelled. "No one in his right mind would be willing to work for so little."

Khiddon reached inside his cloak and brought forth a gold coin. "Excellency," he exclaimed, "I ask you to hold this gold coin for the next two weeks. If the work is not completed by that time, you may keep the coin and pay me nothing for my labors." With this, Khiddon raised his arm high so as to show everyone the glittering piece at his fingertips.

It was at this very instant that Khiura, peering through the curtain, saw the riddle-master.

Khiura had been miserable all morning. It was partly her own fault, for despite her decision not to tell Yidonit about her dream prince she could not keep it a secret—not from Yidonit's piercing eyes. And the fortune-teller gave Khiura a severe tongue-lashing. "If you wish to follow your dreams," she shouted and scolded, "then dream your life away as you please, but come not to me to look into your future." In her anger Yidonit swept the sand and the ashes and feathers and seaweed right off the table, much to the dismay of the birds. At this Khiura broke into tears and promised never, never to dream again. More than that, she gave Yidonit two pieces of gold instead of the usual one. This helped calm the fortune-teller's anger. She even dried Khiura's tears with a kerchief that reeked with overpowering perfume, at which Khiura sneezed mightily and felt much better. "Now," Yidonit ended the visit, "the man *I* see in your future may be a little late coming, but at least he is handsome—not like this—this scarecrow that you keep seeing in your silly dreams."

All the way from Yidonit's house Khiura kept sighing so deeply that the palanquin shook and heaved at every step. The slaves darkly agreed that carrying the palanquin was worse than trying to stand on one leg in a boat during a storm.

Finally Khiura, overcome by her own sighing, decided to have a look around. She parted the curtain and looked out on the market place.

There, arm upraised, the sun shining on his fingertips, was the prince of her dreams!

The most proper thing for Khiura to have done, at that moment, was to faint, and indeed she was about to go into a deep swoon. Then, realizing that the palanquin was moving on past the scene Khiura changed her mind.

"Stop, fools," she screamed at the slaves.

The palanquin came to a jarring halt that almost threw Khiura out through the window curtains.

"That man over there," she panted hoarsely, pointing to Khiddon, "the one next to the boy with long hair. Fetch him hither, immediately!"

At the first sound of Khiura's voice the men in the group surrounding the official turned around sharply. When they saw where the voice was coming from, they split into two groups. The young men made off as fast as their legs could carry them, as though pursued by a plague. Their elders stood still, waiting for what would happen next.

One of Khiura's servants ambled up to Khiddon and bowed low. "My mistress, the most noble Khiura, daughter of Patish the Governor of Ekron, wishes to have a word with you, sir."

"Her father is the one for whom I shall uproot the trees?" whispered Khiddon to the official.

"The same."

Khiddon's face broke out in a broad smile. This was good fortune indeed! Again he turned to the official. "Allow me to assure her that soon she will be looking at a beautiful garden on that spot, and I shall then return to complete our agreement."

The official said nothing, but into his eyes, as he watched Khiddon striding cheerfully behind the slave, there came a look of deep pity.

The riddle-master paused by the curtained window. "My noble lady," he said softly, "it is good of you to have noticed me. I am your humble servant."

"The gods be praised!" came through the curtain. "It is so wonderful!"

The smile faded a bit from Khiddon's lips. Was that the voice of a woman? It sounded more like that of an animal being slowly strangled.

"Enter and sit at my side, O vision of my dreams," the voice continued. The curtain parted a bit, invitingly.

Khiddon looked back at the group behind him. The official's face was most woebegone, but the others were grinning broadly, as though daring him to go ahead.

The riddle-master was not to be cowed easily. He laid his hand on the curtain. "You do me great honor, Princess," he said loudly. "Surely I am not worth it."

Khiura gurgled in sheer delight. This was exactly how her dream prince talked! She reached out and coyly opened the curtain wider.

Khiddon's eyes, as he attempted to pierce the gloom inside the palanquin, told him nothing, but his nose was less fortunate and more informative. A whiff of heavy perfume assailed him and he found himself choking for air, much to the amusement of the others. He braced himself, placed one foot on the palanquin step and nimbly leaped inside, with the mocking cheers of the market place in his ears.

Samson watched the scene curiously. He felt no fear for his friend, who had proven to be a match for any situation, but something in the behavior of those around him suggested that Khiddon might be in some trouble.

The official noticed the look of concern on Samson's face. "Is he a friend of yours?" he whispered kindly.

"We came to Ekron together," was Samson's cautious reply.

"A pity," sighed the official. He turned to the others. "Your attention, please. Because of . . . uhm . . . ah . . . certain unforeseen developments the bid of Shurbosh may yet be accepted. However, nothing is to be done unless and until the herald of Ekron announces it, at noon tomorrow."

The official then turned to Samson. "Do you know where the governor's palace is?" he asked.

Samson shook his head.

The official nodded in the direction of the disappearing palanquin. "Just follow it, young man, just follow it. Your friend will need all the help he can get."

PATISH STOOD at the window of his chamber and stared at the wooded patch below, on the other side of the ravine.

His thoughts were far from pleasant. He had returned, only an hour earlier, from a tour of the Philistine cities. Officially this tour was no more than the usual round of visits which the governors paid each other from time to time. But it was no secret that, wherever Patish now went, it was with the thought of finding a good son-in-law—*any* son-in-law, people whispered knowingly—but to no avail. In the taverns and in the market place it was agreed that a man would have to be blind, deaf, and his nose stuffed with wax to ask for Khiura's hand. Small wonder that the rich rewards promised by Patish found no takers!

Patish stood at the window and angrily tugged at his thick black beard. The gods had refused to give him a son—only a daughter who looked like a bear.

The clicking of the beaded curtain behind him broke into Patish's moody thought. Before he could turn around he was almost bowled over by Khiura's embrace.

"O father, father!" she cried. "I have found him! He is here at last—the prince of my dreams!"

Patish drew back and looked at his daughter sharply. He was beginning to be suspicious of her daily visits with Yidonit.

"It is true!" Khiura went on, gasping like a fish washed ashore. "I found him in the market place, father." Her eyes were glowing like two lumps of hot coal. "He is the image in my dream! He is my hope come true!"

By this time Patish was thoroughly frightened. Surely the gods had stricken his poor daughter with madness! Still he managed to remain outwardly calm. "Where is he of whom you speak, daughter?" he asked gently.

"In the reception hall," replied Khiura, half-dragging her father by his cloak. "Come and give him your blessing."

Khiddon was standing exactly where Khiura had left him. From the moment that he first saw the young woman in broad daylight, the riddle-master acted as though he was fashioned of stone, so stunned was he by what his eyes had seen. Something inside him urged him to flee for his life, but he couldn't move a limb. Besides, the palace guards had shut the gates tight, sensing that Khiura would order them to be hanged if they let Khiddon get away.

Through the haze in his head the riddle-master thought of Samson, and into his heart there came a spark of hope— but only for an instant. How could Samson possibly come to his rescue? The boy probably didn't know where the palanquin had carried off his doomed companion.

Khiura and her father came into the hall. Out of sheer habit Khiddon bowed low, and the act broke the spell. The riddle-master's wits came back to him in one gushing flow.

"Welcome, welcome!" boomed Patish. He took a good look at Khiddon, and his confusion mounted. He had expected to see some freakish sort of fellow, lured by the promise of wealth and high position, but this man was truly handsome. How could Khiura have snared him?

"I thank you indeed, O Governor of Ekron," returned Khiddon, now the soul of charm. "I also thank your beautiful daughter, whose grace has not its equal in all of Philistia."

Khiura gasped and giggled with delight, but her father did not seem at all pleased. This suitor was out of his mind!

"Good, good," snapped Patish. The less he understood what was going on, the angrier he became. "I shall spend the rest of the day at the barracks. We shall talk further at the evening meal."

"Yes, we shall begin making our plans," exclaimed Khiura, gazing at Khiddon with a heavenly rapture that sent chills up and down his spine. He was barely able to keep his legs steady enough to follow a servant to the guest chamber.

Once he found himself alone Khiddon drew aside

the window curtain and looked out on the bright daylight. A scent of flowers filled the warm air, and the merry chirping of birds, gay and free, came from the green woods.

The riddle-master stepped out to the balcony and glanced at the wall surrounding the palace. Something caught his eye—the glint of the sun's rays on something bright at the edge of the ravine. The object moved, and with disbelief Khiddon realized that he was looking at Samson's head!

The riddle-master sighed with relief; at least the boy was safe. But how did he get there? No matter, thought Khiddon. This was the time for action! He measured with his practiced eye the drop from the balcony to the ground below. It was not more than twice his own height. He clambered over the railing, looked about to see that he was not being observed, and dropped to the sandy earth.

The wall, though high, was fashioned of uneven stones and therefore was full of chinks and small openings from top to bottom. Khiddon gave a hoot, two chirps, and another hoot.

"Is that you, Khiddon?" came Samson's voice from the other side of the wall.

The riddle-master put some sand into one of the openings and blew it through. An instant later Samson was peering at him. "What has happened?" the boy asked. "Are you in danger?"

"In such danger as never had threatened a man before," replied Khiddon. Strangely enough there wasn't the slightest hint of worry in his voice. An idea had come to him—an idea so brilliant and ingenious that it almost overpowered him. "Listen closely, Samson," he went on.

"You see the cluster of trees on the other side of the ravine?"

"Indeed I do," the boy replied. "Is this the one—"

"Yes, yes," interrupted Khiddon. "Now bear in mind, Samson, that this is a matter of life and death to one who I trust is dear to you, namely, myself. Yea, it is a matter that can be worse than death, therefore I call on you to do it. You must uproot the trees, cast them across the ravine to form a bridge, and close up the holes—all of this to be done between midnight and dawn. Can you do it, Samson? If not, I shall forever be doomed, as no man has been since the creation of the world."

"It shall be done," Samson replied confidently.

"You have saved my life," Khiddon exclaimed. "May you never know the tortures that I have been going through, this past hour. Now then, go back to the market place and buy something to eat. Here is the money." He took a piece of silver from his pouch and threw it over the wall.

"I have it," Samson called.

"Remember! Do not begin before midnight, and finish by dawn. Then wait for me at the east gate."

The riddle-master barely had time to turn away from the wall when his eye caught sight of a flurry of color coming toward him. It was Khiura, decked out in a gown that suggested a drunken rainbow. Her features matched the gown, having been heavily made up with shades of red, yellow and blue. Khiddon gulped twice.

"Ah, my dear, you are indeed a vision of delight," he exclaimed. "It was indeed my hope that I see you here, midst the flowers which pale beside your beauty."

Khiura gurgled coyly. "I did not find you in your chamber," she murmured, "and I therefore went to look for you." She bent so close to Khiddon that the riddle-master had to stop breathing, fearing that the strong perfume would choke him. He took Khiura by the hand and led her to a stone bench by a honeysuckle bush. "My sweet Princess, light of my life," he began. "Though my heart cries out for you, and though my soul burns with the magic of your love, alas, it cannot be!"

Khiura stared at Khiddon blankly.

"You see, my beloved," continued the riddle-master, every tone dripping with tears, "were I a mortal, like all other men who walked this earth, then would I sweep you up in my arms and you would be mine, forever. But alas! No such good fortune is mine!"

Khiura's lips moved, but not a sound came forth.

"Foolish was I to have allowed myself to be carried away by your charms," the "dream prince" went on, "for well did I know it could not come to pass. Now all that is left for me is to ask your forgiveness and to depart, to return to my abode, where no mortal can set foot."

"W—who are you?" Khiura asked in awe.

"I am born of the gods," replied Khiddon solemnly. "I have been sent, in mortal guise, to seek out the ways of men and to observe their deeds. To the gods I must now return, for so have they decreed. Tomorrow at sunrise I must depart, never to be seen again."

At this, Khiura burst into sobs so loud that Khiddon expected to see the palace guards come running. "There, now," he cried soothingly, "we must not lose hope."

Khiura raised her head, and Khiddon's jaw dropped. The tears had caused the colors on the girl's cheeks to run together. "Hope?" she repeated weakly.

"Yes," replied Khiddon. "Let us return to our chambers, you to yours and I to mine. There we shall pray to the gods that I be allowed to keep my human form, for I would rather have you for a wife than be one of the gods."

Nothing more was said until the two entered the palace. There Khiddon, head bowed in great sorrow, took leave of Khiura and hurried to his chamber. He lay down on the couch, completely worn out, and immediately fell asleep.

It was no more than an hour later that the riddle-master was shaken out of his slumber. He opened his eyes and looked straight into the wrathful countenance of Patish.

The Governor of Ekron yanked his guest up from the couch like a sack of meal. "What is all this nonsense you have been telling my daughter, scoundrel?" he roared. "A son of the gods you be?"

Khiddon sighed. Every move now had to be made with extreme care. "It is true, O noble Patish," he replied sadly. "When the Princess invited me to join her in her carriage I had no idea that—"

"—that you would have to marry her, eh?" snarled Patish.

Again Khiddon sighed. "I am sorry the Princess related to you what I told her, but it is the truth."

"Indeed!" cried Patish, knotting his huge fists. "I shall beat you until your skin hangs in tatters. Then we shall know what you are, man or god!"

Khiddon did not flinch. "Do not tempt nor anger me,

O Patish," he cried, "lest with a wave of my hand I reduce your palace to ashes and your power to dust." Then his voice softened. "Yet I cannot blame you, O Governor of Ekron, for your show of doubt. I am indeed the first one born of the gods to appear among men. Therefore I must give you a true sign, one that will remove the doubt from your heart. After I partake of the evening meal— for I must act as one of you while I abide here—I shall either prove to you that I am of the gods or I shall gladly marry your daughter."

Patish's dark mood left him at once. This rascal was indeed insane, to pretend that he was one of the gods! But better a man with strange fancies than no husband at all! "Let us go to our evening meal," he exclaimed jovially. "I promise you that it will be fit for the gods—or their sons."

Khiddon bowed low and followed his host to the dining room.

"This wine," said Patish, as he faced Khiddon across the low table, with Khiura at his side, "came from the island of Crete, where my fathers lived before they settled here on the shores of the Great Sea." He took a long sip and smacked his lips loudly. "As one of my wedding gifts to you and your wife I shall give you a fine sailing vessel, and the two of you will visit Crete. What say you to that?"

Khiddon shook his head sadly. "Your generous offer merely deepens the sadness in my heart, O noble Patish," he said. "Would that I were like all men."

Patish reared back in anger. "Enough of this!" he bellowed. "Give me a sure sign of your godly powers, *now*, or I shall have your tongue pulled out of your head!"

Khiura, who had been matching her father bite for bite and gulp for gulp, gave a cry of distress. The thought of her dream prince without a tongue was more than she could bear. Without a word she rose and ran to her room, sobbing loudly.

As for the riddle-master, the threat of the wrathful Patish seemed to affect him not in the least. Slowly he rose and stepped toward the balcony. Immediately Patish was at his side; he was not going to give the wily stranger a chance to jump down and escape from the palace grounds.

The sun had already set. Dusk was deepening into the gloom of night. Arms folded across his chest, Khiddon took up an imposing stand at the balcony railing.

"Through the veil of evening's shadows," he began in a light chant, "I behold the world at rest. I look forth and see the secrets of the heavens and the earth. I hear the wind, carefree, swift, rustling past by yonder trees. I say to the wind: 'I who am come from the gods can still your rustling sound, and it shall not be heard again.' And the wind gives answer: 'True it is that of the gods you are. Yet they who bore you have also fashioned me, the wind, to rustle through the trees and sweep across both plain and desert, to howl through the mountain passes. How then will you stop me?' So speaks the wind."

Khiddon paused. Through his half-closed eyes he could see Patish watching him intently. The riddle-master took up his chant once more.

"Then to the wind I say: 'O wind, how can you rustle where there are no trees? For if I but stretch forth my hand, the trees shall uproot themselves and in their stead bare ground shall be, a garden plot where flowers shall merely nod when you will caress their heads.' Thus I speak, yet the wind rustles on, not believing me." He turned to Patish. "Do *you* believe me, O Governor of Ekron?"

Patish moistened his lips but said nothing.

"Let this then be the sign you seek," continued Khiddon. "My hand I shall stretch forth and bid the trees uproot themselves; nay more, the holes they make they should smooth over, and then stretch their trunks across the ravine. Tomorrow, ere the sun will rise, you will stand here again and tell me what you see. If the stand of trees your eyes will greet, then indeed a mortal am I, and the husband of Khiura I will be. But if your eyes behold naught but bare ground, it is the sign that from the gods am I, and to their abode I must return."

Patish tugged at his thick black beard. Khiddon's words had shaken him. "If you are indeed one of the gods," he said slowly, "and therefore cannot marry my daughter, why have you aroused false hope within her heart? It is enough that every day she goes to see Yidonit, may Dagon curse that witch!"

"It is true that I have led your daughter to believe my words, but so have the gods ordained it," returned Khiddon. "Yet there is a purpose in all this, as you shall soon see, and the Princess will be the happier for it." He turned to the open balcony. "And now, I stretch forth my hand and say: 'O trees, dawn will find you all uprooted. O wind, dawn will find your rustling stilled, as the night is my witness.' And now, O noble Patish, it is time for bed."

The hours passed slowly for Patish. Twice he arose and went out on the balcony. He could see nothing, for it was a moonless night. He listened for the rustling of the wind. The sound seemed to become louder, angrier at first. Was it possible that the wind was having a battle with the powers of the stranger in the adjoining chamber? It was indeed a badly confused ruler of Ekron who finally fell into a fitful, brooding sleep.

Khiddon slept soundly. Ah, that Samson! Never was there such a one, and never would there be another. And Khiddon prayed that he would see the day when the boy, grown to manhood, would return to Philistia to carry out his mission for his people's freedom.

Dawn was just breaking when the riddle-master awoke. He flung aside the sheepskin cover and hurried to the balcony.

A gray mist was sweeping past the palace, hiding everything beyond the wall below. Then, as the sun began to break through from the east, the mist began to lift. The ravine soon became visible, and Khiddon at once knew that he had nothing to fear. Neatly laid out across the ravine, the moist soil still clinging to their bare roots, were the trees that had stood on the tract beyond it only a few hours earlier. Of the wind there was no sound.

A harsh cry interrupted Khiddon's pleasant thoughts. Behind him stood Patish, his eyes bloodshot and mouth wide open. The impossible had happened!

"The wind is stilled, gone forever," chanted Khiddon, "and so shall I be, O Patish. Yet first I shall fulfill the promise of the gods. Awaken your daughter and bring her hither to this chamber, so that I may bestow upon her the blessings of the gods."

As soon as Patish left the room, Khiddon tore off a piece of parchment from the scroll he carried and wrote something on it. When Khiura and her father entered they found the riddle-master at the balcony, his arms upraised as though in prayer for the smooth piece of ground beyond the wall.

"I bring you good tidings, O Princess," said Khiddon, turning toward the two. "I have asked a favor of the gods, and they have granted it." He lifted the palm of his hand so that it moved in front of Khiura's face. "As I have made the trees disappear, so shall other things vanish. Only you must promise me, O Princess, in the presence of your esteemed father, that you will obey my commands as I give them to you this day, for if you do not, never will a male mortal let his eyes rest upon you."

"She will, she will," blurted out Patish, before his daughter could utter a word.

Khiddon turned on him sharply. "It is for your daughter to reply," he said.

"I shall obey, every word," whispered Khiura.

"So be it then," went on Khiddon. "Be true to your promise and the gods will keep theirs. One hour after I take my leave you will summon your most trusted servant and send him to the market place. There he will obtain a measure of such herbs as I have written on this piece of parchment. You, O Princess, will then grind, by your own hand, all the herbs together until they become as fine as dust. To this you will add as much water as would fill half an eggshell. Before every meal you will take a pinch of this paste of herbs and swallow it. When this is gone, send for more and proceed with it as you will have done with the first measure. Are my words clear?"

Khiura and her father nodded.

"This you shall do for three months. During this time you are to drink nothing but water. Also, during this time you are not to leave the palace, nor shall anyone come to see you."

"For three months?" repeated Khiura.

"Hah! This is fine!" exclaimed Patish with glee. "At least you will not be seeing that witch Yidonit every day."

"No one is to see you," repeated Khiddon. "Nor are you to adorn your face with paint or powder." He turned to Patish. "At the end of three months you are to invite all the chieftains of Philistia and their grown sons to a feast, to meet the beautiful girls of Ekron, whom you shall also invite. Then, at the height of the merriment you will bring Princess Khiura into the banquet hall."

A rosy glow came to Khiura's cheeks. "And then?" she whispered.

"And then," proclaimed Khiddon grandly, "there will be silence. The young men will stare at you, and someone will say: 'Can this beauty be Khiura, the daughter of Patish?' At this the young men will press forward, each striving to be the first to ask your father for your hand."

Patish kept staring at Khiddon in amazement. "Can I believe my ears?" he cried hoarsely.

"So have the gods agreed to favor the Princess," returned the riddle-master, "for thus have I bargained with them, since I cannot have the Princess for my own.

It is to this end that I have been sent to Ekron, to rid the Princess from an evil spell that has caused her beauty to be hidden all these years."

"Yidonit!" cried Patish in a rage. "I shall have her hanged!"

"None of that!" returned Khiddon imperiously. "We of the gods do not vie with witches and such. But bear in mind that if my orders are disobeyed, the evil spell will never depart."

Patish was now all smiles. "Bid farewell to the one sent by the gods," he said to his daughter, "then leave us here alone."

Her eyes shining like stars, and with a fond last look at Khiddon, Khiura left the chamber. At the same time Patish went to an iron box in his own room and came back with a small sack in his hands.

"I—I do not know whether one offers a gift of money to the gods," he began. "If all this does come to pass as you have said—"

Khiddon raised his hand sternly. "One does not pay for happiness with money, O Patish," he said. "In three months your daughter will be a beautiful maiden, and beauty cannot be bought. However," he continued, "many a good deed can be done with gold coins. I shall therefore accept your gift, in return for having cleared the trees yonder." He strode toward the balcony and looked out, well aware that Patish had left the room. The riddle-master knew the reason, for one glance at the sack had told him that the coins it contained were of silver. And indeed, when Patish returned the sack in his hand was much smaller—but the coins were of gold.

He thrust the sack into Khiddon's hands and stood there, tears of happiness running down his bearded face.

"One last word," said Khiddon, "and I shall depart. Should anyone ask you, three months hence and beyond, how it was that your daughter became so beautiful, not one word of the reason are you to give in reply. That must always remain my riddle."

"Do YOU really believe that Patish's daughter will ever be beautiful?" asked Samson.

The two companions were moving north, out of Philistine territory, astride two vigorous mules that Khiddon had purchased in the market place of Ekron.

"Indeed I do," returned Khiddon. "Do not forget that I come from Gilead, where one learns to perform miracles with herbs." He smiled faintly. "When we were having our evening meal yesterday," he continued, "I noticed that Khiura ate and drank like her father. Small wonder that she is of abundant flesh and hairy of skin! I therefore ordered that she drink naught but water, which is good for the skin, and that she keep away from paint, which is not. But it is the mixture of herbs that will perform the miracle."

"Speak further, O riddle-master from Gilead," exclaimed Samson jokingly.

"I shall, O strong one of Zor'ah," laughed Khiddon. "The mixture is well-known in Gilead. When swallowed, even a small mouthful, before a meal, it causes the desire to eat to vanish; food becomes sickening, and Cretan wine tastes like vinegar. Yes, in three months our Khiura will have shed many measures of flesh. She will then be as a flower, and many bees shall swarm about her, I assure you."

For a while the two rode on in silence. At a bend in the road, just as Ekron was about to vanish from sight, Khiddon motioned to his companion to halt his mule.

"We are leaving Philistia, Samson," the riddle-master said quietly. "Some day, when the time will come for you to lift the Philistine yoke from your people, you will be coming back here—to Gaza, Timna, perhaps to the Sorek River. You know something about the Philistines now, Samson. They are people like others, but like their gods and idols they have no greatness in them, and in time they shall vanish from the face of the earth. See therefore to the welfare of your people, with whom the Lord has made a covenant, to give them this land for an inheritance and His law for a blessing, for all time."